ari

The Epic Story of the Other Man

ari

Book 2

Published in the United States
by Fact & Fiction LLC

ISBN 978-1-7362884-5-0
eBook ISBN 978-1-7362884-4-3

Edited by Kate Seger
Interior Design by Eli Neff Akridge
Cover Design by Victorine Lieske

www.bccowling.com

REPETITION

LOSS OF DETERMINATION

SURPRISE

THE MAN WAS YOU

GARBAGE AND BLISS

APOLOGIZING NOT GROWING

ANOTHER CHALLENGE

FEELINGS AND FAILURES

WHERE DO YOU WANT TO GO?

PERHAPS AS ROBERT DID

ODD JOBS

UNFALLEN TEARS

RUNNING ON EMPTY

FOREVER

AT HER LIMIT

I DON'T KNOW

UNDERSTANDING

YES

HUSH

HAPPY BIRTHDAY

NEEDING REASSURANCE

WHY'S THAT?

HOPE SURGING

HOPE DASHED

AROUND THE CORNER AND ACROSS THE STREET

BEYOND REASON

TOO FAR ALREADY?

LOST POSSESSIONS

WHAT DO I THINK?

HOW CAN I DO ANYTHING BUT LOVE HER?

HOPE

SCARED OF MY ANGER

MAYBE I WILL

BACK TOWARD LOVE

PATH TO FREEDOM

WORDS THAT WOUND

A DREAM OF GIBBERISH

SEX OR ALCOHOL

A SURPRISE

CURIOUSLY MISSING URGENCY

LONGING FOR SIMPLICITY

LOVE AND RISK

STAYING CAUSE

MAMILANI

SHE COMES TO YOU FOR LOVE

KIND NECESSARY & TRUE

LOVE AND TRUST AND LOSS

I WOULD NOT MIND

WITH RICH BUSH CLINTON AND PEROT

ANOTHER SAD SUNDAY

REPETITION

Four and a half days I've been home
I can call it home once again
An empty home
Without Ari in town

Sixty hours of dragging one leg past the other
Flopping its foot down anywhere it will land
Then the other
Steps
Taking little steps with great effort
Keeping my focus straight ahead
If I look to the side I lose my momentum
In an instant

My fifth day of writing
Not so much that I am consumed with it
Not so much to get dangerously high on the creative flow
Not so much to drain my tired body
But enough to build upon

Work is like starting over again
A few loans still in the pipeline
Enough to meet basic expenses for this month
And perhaps next
Not enough to pay for the Paris trip
Without going further in debt
Not enough to pay for the next trip upfront
No want for incentive to re-establish my pipeline of loans
No want for incentive to work toward taking it to a new level

Placed an ad yesterday for a marketing assistant
To be paid for out of savings
I have savings!
The remainder of money borrowed
For the down payment on my new car

Which I never bought

A good time for repetition
Waiting for Ari to come home

LOSS OF DETERMINATION

Heavy tears in the middle of the night
Waking in a sweat
Hours after having laid down for a nap
Tired
Too tired to get up

Missing Ari terribly in my blackness
Laureen not having returned my calls from yesterday
Neither Michelle nor Colleen nor Scott
Or anyone else calling me back

Me the one who calls
Me the one so wrapped up in my life
In Ari
Seldom having time for other friends when they call
Which never was very often
Now is never

Feeling so alone
So abandoned
Why can't I shake this?
Why do I go on dragging such misery with me?
Spilling it occasionally or often onto those I love
Onto Ari

At work
Pouring sweetness onto Margie
Our company's number three
Wanting my number two
Or at least co-number two
Getting back sourness and ill-humor
No fun
Normally only a small problem
Today with Ari still gone it got to me
Tonight another black hole in my sky of darkness

The tears and sobbing came without let-up
Until my chest wheezed and a coughing spasm stretched
Beyond a few minutes

Crying the cry of the deeply wounded
Hearing Ari tell me so many things that would kill me
That she doesn't love me anymore
That Robert demands she doesn't see me anymore
That she can't handle my pain anymore
That she isn't coming home
That she doesn't love me anymore

My mind isn't to be trusted
When I am so vulnerable
So alone
Feeling so alone
Unable to open to Spirit
To the companion who never wavers
To my spiritual guide
To the Mahanta

Closed from too many days without Ari
Closed from not being able to find the strength
To remain open to serve others
No matter what I feel

My determination a fading retina image
Of hues seen when I was able to open my eyes last
Gasping for breath
In the too-thin atmosphere of living without Ari

SURPRISE

I sat at my desk looking out the window
Having just called home
Two rings telling me there was no message on my machine
For perhaps the tenth time in six hours

I wondered how much longer I could force myself to work
But did not want to go home
Did not want to go anywhere

I felt the urge rise to call Ari's store
Pushed it away
She was still in Los Angeles
Or at best on a plane over the Pacific
I wanted to hear from her by the evening at the latest
Needed desperately to hear from her
Expecting she would tell me she had to stay in LA
To buy for the store
Hoping it would only be for a day or two
Fearing it might be Saturday before I saw her

I heard her voice on the phone in my mind
It was the evening
She was home having skipped LA
Telling me she was beat
Asking me if I would forgive her
If she did not come over that evening

"I will forgive you anything" I said in my mind

The phone rang
I heard Yeo's voice grow warmer in recognition
"Sure he's here
   Just a minute
   Zak Ari is on the phone"

My heart leaped

I grabbed the phone and said
Almost groaning
"Oh I was just thinking about you"

She laughed her wonderful laugh
"You must have heard me thinking of you"
Said she was downtown
I asked her to come by
She said she would be there in ten minutes

I danced around my desk
Feeling a horrendous weight lift
Checked the computer and printer
In the middle of a long run

Not willing to waiting until the printing was finished
I asked Yeo to watch it
Told her I would be waiting for Ari out front
To come get me if she called again unexpectedly

The sunshine felt wonderful
I leaned against a street light
One foot propped up in back on the base

Millions and millions of cars went by on King Street
On this Wednesday afternoon
She was longer in coming than ten minutes
Not at her best with timing and traffic

But she came
Pulling to a stop in front of me
In the silver Volvo wagon with a large box in back
One of three from customs I guessed
Since I had learned from Gudren that
Only one of the three missing Visas had arrived
In the last shipment from Bali
Still held-up at US Customs

Ari glowed with Beauty
Wearing the black top and the green checked pants
She had arrived in Paris wearing

"Take me to my place" I said
She nodded and asked me several questions about
My trip back
My health
My work
The writing

"I don't think I can talk until I kiss you"
The little peck on her cheeks and lips
A kiss to neither of us

We drove the few blocks to my apartment in silent rapture
Holding hands
Touching arms necks shoulders
She having difficulty keeping her eyes on driving
Me unable to look anywhere except at her

The moment felt almost awkward
Like the first thirty seconds at the train station in Paris
When she arrived

Then she was parking in my parking stall
We took the elevator up one floor
Hugging full body
I almost ran to my door
To open it quickly knowing she would wait at the stairs
Not wanting to stand exposed at my door
Exposed to heavy traffic on Punahou Street
The thousands of people she and Robert know
Driving by each day waiting to catch her
At another man's home

I unlocked the door turning back to her as I opened it
Found her right behind me pushing me into the kitchen

Where we kissed and held each other as lovers
For the first time in more than seven days

I asked her if she minded being ravished
"I want to brush my teeth first" she smiled
We both brushed our teeth
Then were on my bed in each other's arms
Rolling
Laughing
Looking deeply into each other's eyes

My heart was happy though a little guarded
We both knew she would have to leave soon

"I thought you would have to stay in LA for the store"
"I had to sort out the Visas and
   I couldn't wait to see you"

I was so sure she would stay in LA
Putting good sense ahead of the longing in her heart
Not at all sure I would

I swept away the silly thought and kissed her
We melted together as we do so well
She telling me in between kisses
Robert and the girls
Had met her on the train three stops early
She being awakened by squeals of "Mommy! Mommy!"

I ask how Robert was
"Fine just fine
   I am okay with Robert"
I did not ask exactly what that meant
Instead wanted to know how he was with us
"It doesn't bother him"
"And what do you think of that?"
"It puzzles me
   I am taking nothing for granted"

"And how are you with us?" I asked
"Full of love"

I saw her smiling with her heart through her eyes
Thought to myself
"She's okay with Robert and full of love for me
   I'll settle for that"
Asked her the always dreaded question in Honolulu
Just now remembered
"How much time do you have"
"I'd better leave soon
   I have so much work to do"
Kissing her I said
"I may not let you go soon"

THE MAN WAS YOU

She did leave
Not soon but an hour later
Stopping by a bakery on the way to my office
Me tagging along
Feeling funny as she brought bread for her other husband
The one she spends most of her time with

We said good-bye with the deepest of warmth
But quickly
She driving off to work and home
I walking upstairs glad to find Bob still there
Feeling drained relieved elated and a little unsettled

In Honolulu before she left for Europe
We were together often
But always for short times
Except when Robert and the kids were all out of town

In Paris we lived together every moment of six days
As in Bali
But different
Our hearts were not scheduled to be ripped out
When our Paris time ended
Ripping mine out when Ari left on the train
Was my choice
Not because of realities to be faced in Honolulu

But now I did face the realities of Honolulu
Ari leaving so quickly
Not staying with me

Having her back was a loss in itself
Adjusting to being the other man
Realizing Robert is her husband
I am the other husband at best
Perhaps only a transient lover

I shook off these thoughts
Plunged into a marketing discussion with Bob
Brought in dinner later
Spending the evening at the office
Doing only a little work
Thinking of Ari
While I got used to the idea of working evenings
Got used to the idea of seeing her sporadically

Eating Thai food at the extra desk in the office
I remembered telling Ari about Pigalle
Telling her how happy I was
I had not subjected her to such garbage
"I knew if I asked you not to go
   And if you still felt pulled to go
   You would have some unfinished business in Paris
   I'm glad it worked out" she said amazing me

I thought about why she and I are together as we are
Remembered her telling me as we were in the bathroom
Just before she left my apartment earlier
That she had finished a book by The Path's spiritual leader
We both were reading
A timely book for me
"I finished *Lessons Of The Heart*
   It's wonderful
   I feel like I'm stepping into the next phase of The Path
   I feel so eager so hungry"

After watching her go through her first burst of excitement
Over finding The Path
Watching her become more aware of her dreams
Watching Spirit move so quickly in her outer life
Listening to her recount her experiences
Especially the little parts of life we all have
The way Spirit teaches us if we can see it
A few of her experiences grand ones

Beyond anything I have an awareness of

Then watching her slide into an undefined disappointment
As she was left on her own by Spirit
To live what she creates
Spirit giving so much
That when It leaves us momentarily to just our own creations
The aloneness can be devastating

Ari got a small taste of this
A small test by Spirit
Hearing her tell me of her renewed excitement
I saw she had passed the test
Something no one could do for her
Had found her next step on The Path

I reminded myself what my role was for her
To help clear The Path
I learned in one workshop at the Seminar in Paris
That in doing this for her and others
I am better able to shed the Passions of the Mind
Lust Greed Vanity Anger Attachment
And the better I am able to help

As I sat with these thoughts
A little blue star twinkled in my peripheral vision
Vanishing as soon as I looked for it
I felt Spirit fill me with
Love and Gratitude
Balancing for the moment
My attachments and needs

Then I remembered Ari's dream she shared with me
"I was undergoing a test of six attributes
    With a man
    Needed to be in a relationship
    Trust
    Kindness

Communication
Some others
And Making Love which had to be done in front of others
Had to be approved by them
We made love in front of the townspeople
And were approved
The man was you"

I remembered the bubbling grin on her face when she repeated
"The man was you" then added
"I feel we are being tested in our relationship"

My heart soared with the memory
"Did this mean we really would be together
In this lifetime?" I asked myself
Floating on happiness with the thought
Knowing nothing was ever certain
Not giving the thought center stage
I headed home
My apartment again home now that Ari was back

GARBAGE AND BLISS

The next workday passed without hearing from Ari
I would like for that not to bother me
It did

Laying at home in the evening
Unable to rest
Wrestling with my little boy
Demanding attention
Demanding love

The phone rang
It was her calling to say she was at her shop working
I offered to come down
She said "We can have a drink"
"We're drinking now?"
"What do you mean?" she asked
The little joke died
Its lightness stamped out by the tone in my voice
My edge of discomfort looking for someone to blame

She looked tired and harried when I got there
Bending over a pile of bags
Bending under the pressures
Of catching up on a month of paperwork
For her store
For their chain of salons
Preparing to move the following week

I helped her carry boxes back out to her car
Feeling slighted
Unhappy she had not called earlier
To let me know she might be able to see me
Feeling unhappy too
That I could not just go with the best she could do

"Gudren is here

She's been helping" Ari told me
Which meant there would be no alone time with her
My gut twitched

I began making little digging comments
Smiling to cover my pain and anger until she told me
Robert had asked her to not go out in the evenings
Until after they moved
Then I could not smile

"He worries about every little thing"

She was so tired she was a little giddy
My mewling and puking rolled off her back as she
Laughed at me with love
Somewhere I found the awareness to stop throwing garbage
And told her how hard it was for me not to have any idea
When she might or might not pop-up in my life
Especially hard when I could not call her
Or make plans with her

She kissed my cheek and said
"When I am with him I miss you
When I am with you I do not miss him
That should help"
"That does not help!" I yelled
But it did help
I was being a brat

She took me by the hand and led me out of the parking garage
Toward her shop
Touching me until we were too near the store to risk it

Gudren came back from talking to a friend
To ask what else she could do
We went to have a snack and some tea
Somehow I pulled myself out of my black hole and
Did a good job of keeping the conversation moving

Ari wanting to be alone as much as I but
Wanting more not to be obvious
Gudren was lost in her latest boyfriend disaster and
A little left out of our conversation until
I worked to include her in it

Later in the evening Ari and I found an excuse
To go out to the car alone again
Leaving Gudren talking with a friend at a nearby cafe
We shared a few minutes of tenderness
Which made possible my cheerful goodbye
To them both a little later

The next day Ari called in the afternoon
To tell me she could go to class that evening
Would be running errands and could pick-up me up at home
"Great
   I'll leave the parking space for you"

The rest of my work day flew by
Grateful she had let me know her plans

When she drove up
I left the door ajar and
Hid behind the kitchen counter
Then surprised her when she walked in
By swooping her into my arms and carrying her to the bed

Happy I did not throw out my back
I dropped her onto the bed expecting her to bounce
Forgetting I had a cotton-stuffed futon
She yelled that her insides were mush
But still grinned and reached up to me
We had half an hour before
Needing to leave for Laureen's class

We rolled and tickled and kissed

So hungry for each other
Passed the fever of first seeing each other on Wednesday
After a week apart
Passed my snit the day before
"You called me ahead of time today
   Thanks" I told her looking into the eyes of Beauty
"I learned a lesson yesterday"

She kissed me
The time to leave for class passed without fanfare
We decided to do a spiritual exercise instead
When the class was to start
Make love
Then go out for Korean food

We sat facing each other
Holding hands
A small joke of mine about
What kind of vehicle I was declaring myself to be
Set off twenty minutes of laughter
Before we settled into a long HHHHUUUUUU

After the exercise she said
"I was riding a white horse
   Through the most amazing blue and gold light
   I feel so clean and light
   Like I could almost float now"

We laughed and glowed together
Both feeling the light
I told her of Sri Thomas
Taking my hand after our HU
How she had taken my other hand
Then Thomas' wife Arlean had taken his hand and
Just as she was about to join with Ari to form a circle
Rebazar Tars had appeared between them
Taking both their hands and
Smiling his regal smile full of love and humility

Had bowed to us all
Then led us in the Hokey Pokey

I told Ari how seeing him so full of fun
His maroon robe swirling
As he put one leg in
Then put one leg out
Doing the Hokey Pokey as we all danced about
Seeing this Master of such wisdom
Who is often so direct in sharing his message
My heart burst open
Feeling the tiny demands of my little self exposed
By his willingness to serve Spirit in any way

I undressed Ari slowly
Playing and teasing
Promising her something special
Both of us so happy
I laid a sheet on the bed
Then gave her a slippery oil massage until she purred
I declaring August "Pamper Ari Month"
She did not protest

Finishing her massage a long while later
She laying on her tummy
I gently pulled her hips into the air
Made sure she was comfortable
Then began lightly licking all over her bottom
Which I learned she liked in Paris
Liked a lot
Learned the last night we were together
Making a mental note to devote more effort to this pleasure

Our lovemaking eventually followed
Such intense pleasure and sharing
We floated on a fluffy bed of light and love
Until it was far too late for Korean food
Finally showering together

She leaving for home and Robert
Me walking back upstairs from watching her drive off
To the bed we shared for the evening
Our time in Paris still so close in my mind
I had difficulty understanding
Why she wasn't still there with me
Her final words to me of the evening
Echoing in my mind

After I had said to her as we stood beside her car
"Your smile lights up my heart
  Your kiss banishes my good sense"
She looked into my eyes and said
"Then kiss me a little more"

APOLOGIZING NOT GROWING

I floated through Saturday
Working at the office after being stood-up
By aspiring telemarketers
Surprised at lunch just after ordering
By Ari's page from home

We had a quick talk
She having to cover for an employee that evening
Between five and seven
I planned to meet her there
Then dared to ask her about afterwards
She had plans with Robert and
I threw away our harmony in a heartbeat of petulance

Our talk stretched into a long pull of my disappointment
My jealousy of her with Robert instead of me
Of her depression at my constant pulling
"You're never satisfied" she told me
"That's right" I said thinking
"And I won't be until we're married"
But kept the thought to myself
Not wanting to expose a hope so dear
To her rising anger

I finally regained my good sense and apologized
Which she did not receive gracefully
We hung up in mid-air
I returned to my lunch bringing budding regret to the table

After another non-sleeping nap
I bought some flowers
Not sure of how she would receive them
Not sure how I felt

When I walked into her shop a little later
She beamed

Really happy to see me and the flowers
Smelling the vase full of little pink rosebuds
Touching the blooming red rose in the middle

"I thought you were not coming
Tired of me and the situation"
I was speechless
And asked her what the two things I get upset about
She thought then said
"Me not expressing my feeling
And not seeing me enough"
"Right
Now how often have I griped about seeing you too much?"
"Never"
"And how often have I complained
About doing something boring with you"
"Never"
"Right
Please keep that in mind next time you think
I am getting tired of you"
She smiled and I kissed her
When she bent down behind the counter

Her worker did not come in at all
Ari had to cancel with Robert
Leaving him to have dinner with their friend alone
"Was he as pissy as me when I don't get to see you?"
I said her after she hung up from calling him
She nodded and smiled
Seeing the humor
Feeling the strain

We spent all evening together in her shop
At one point I told her of my silent response
To her jab that I was never satisfied
Then asked her
"How does it feel to have someone wanting to marry you
So badly?"

"Wonderful since it is you
   And a little unrealistic for now"
"For now" she had said in a whisper
I repeated the two words and she nodded

"All I know is that I have watched myself change so much
   In the last two years
   I don't know what is happening tomorrow
   I can make any promises"
I heard her words and felt her say silently to me
"If I keep changing
   I may not be able to stay with Robert
   No matter how much I want to keep the family together
   But I don't dare say it now"

Was I running off a cliff
Looking back at this kite of my own presumption
Flying high overhead?
I did not know

She told me she had decided to abandon
Four dresses at Customs
To get the rest of the shipment freed now
Without waiting for the final re-worked visa
To arrive from the shipper in Bali

I asked quietly what the prospects were
For her escort to accompanying her
She said "Pretty good"
I probed and she told me
Robert had asked her if she had "promised him yet"
To go to St. Louis to the next Seminar in October
Wanting to be reasonable she told him
She would probably not go
Because her next trip would be about the same time
To Bali and Thailand she hoped

She then told Robert I wanted to go with her to Bali again

He did not object strongly but raised his hands
In an unclear expression which could have meant
"I give up" or "What nerve" or "Shoot me"
“How can he afford this?" Robert had asked
I wondered that too
As I heard Ari recount the conversation
But did not flinch
Glad that only one trip was planned for the fall
Determined to build my business
So I could keep traveling with her
If the window stayed open
Cautioning myself not to count on it

The rest of the evening was marred
Only by my honesty when she asked
If I minded if she went out to the car for a nap
She asked this after suggesting I go home for a nap
Knowing how tired I was still not caught-up from my jet lag
Even though I had been home nine days

I wasn't thrilled standing around in her store
But could not bear to be away from her
Knowing I was passing up time with her

I knew I would be resentful if left alone in the store
And could not find the grace
To look after the shop for a while

"Yes I mind
  But I will do it"

She did not take me up on my offer
Even after I pushed her to do so

As the evening wore on I regretted my childishness
I apologized with my heart
When we left late after closing

Having missed our Korean dinner
From the night before
Again
She was loving and gracious in accepting
I felt hypocritical
Getting better at apologizing than growing

We parked for a while on the way to another restaurant
Then decided not to eat and
Went to the top of our favorite parking garage nearby
Spending an hour flirting with sleep
Then touching tenderly

She drove me back to my car
Leaving to my concern
Of her staying awake on her way home
Our hearts fully open and one

ANOTHER CHALLENGE

The little boy spoke again today
Putting myself the adult in an ignoble position
Not a new situation
I am not a very noble person
I try hard to be real
As real as I can be
Putting my truest self on the table
Sometimes this creates laughter and fun
Sometimes the pile of bloody intestines
Which is me in that moment
Drips onto the floor

Today was both

Ari and I met at the Center for Sunday Service
Had lunch by ourselves
Then were joined by other friends

Went to her new house to make a list of needed supplies
Before doing several household repairs
We waited for Robin to come to discuss cleaning
Robert arrived instead
Running late getting keys made
We unloaded the station wagon full of boxes
Seeing each other for the first time in over four months

Not since the Tuesday night "interview"
Long ago in early April
Pre-Bali
Pre-Paris
Pre-the fragile status quo of today

He was civil but not friendly
More gracious than I would have been
But not the man who said to Ari before the trip to Europe
"Tell Zak I am sorry I was not friendlier to him

When he called"
This said after the one time I had called their house
When Ari asked me to find out something
And he answered the phone
He sounded busy the way he said "Here she is"
Which is what he used to say
Before the shit hit the fan at the end of March

It was a hands-off situation for me this afternoon
Not wanting to make any waves
Knowing my existence taxed his life enough

I was polite and neutral
Maybe friendly
But I did not want to see him
Any more than he wanted to see me

My primary concern was that he would stick around and
Ruin—for me—our planned afternoon together
He did not
Even though he returned with more boxes
After Robin had come and gone

Ari went through a hard time after he left
Seeing us both together
Seeing him in such pain at leaving she and I together
I could not do what is he is doing

I tried to give her the forum and support
To talk through her feelings
And she did!
Delighting me
As she opened up with seeming ease

We mixed work and play for the next several hours
At her new home
At several stores
At my apartment

Rushing back to her new house to finish
Before we lost the light
After spending an hour or more
Changing her clothes at my home

The work was done in a flurry ending with us both tired
I wanted to have a relaxed dinner with her
In our world of often-manufactured reasons to be together
Reasons which enabled her to maintain
Some balance at home with Robert while seeing me

"I am going to spend the afternoon with Zak" not workable

The day's accomplishments seemed a perfect excuse
"He worked for us all day
  Now I am going to take him to dinner"
That proposition was very compelling
After helping Ari with her new store
Just a month before

Instead she said
"I feel guilty leaving Robert alone all day
  Knowing he is there alone and hurting
  I feel I need to go home"

I could have been gracious and supportive
I could have been neutral
I could have been extremely shitty
I was none of the above
But I was closer to shitty than neutral

My little boy decided he was deeply offended that
She would worry about Robert being alone
When I am alone so much more than Robert is

So we spent enough time to have a nice dinner together
Pulling and tugging at each other
Getting a little heated at times

She more weary than hot
I more annoyed than angry

We did not solve anything
We parted in just-regained harmony without eating
Perhaps understanding ourselves and each other a little more
She mostly tired and beaten
I gyrating with great vigor to stay on my razor's edge
Of juggling reason clarity and love
With my emotional herd of wild horses
With my little boy

We did highlight a challenge that
Perhaps I can postpone no longer

In relationships I have often given away my personal space
To be very close to someone
To satisfy my little boy needs

I have known this for several years
Learning it undeniably
Over three relationships in five years in which
I was miserably vulnerable
Not taking care of myself

With Ari I have an excuse to not deal with this
She is available to me only a few hours a week
Not hours we can plan for
Often simply there at the end of the phone
Saying she has some time carved out in her busy schedule

What do I do?
If I am not available I miss seeing her
Those possible hours together gone forever and
Maybe she won't have an opening again for a day or two

If I take care of the business of my life first
Then I am miserable when she calls and I am tied up

So I work hard to be ready at almost all times
Which means I give away a lot of space

She told me tonight
She would like to hear me say once in a while when she calls
"I can't break free just now
How about in a couple of hours"

I got angry when I heard that
Of course she would like to hear me say that
I would not like to hear her always say
"Anytime you like"
I would feel like she had no life of her own
And would feel threatened and cramped

But

In our situation
When I cannot call her to talk
Or ask her out for the evening
Or make plans
Or see her a little later because I am working now

I bend the way I easily bend
And pay the price

She said in response to my objection that
She is never around a couple of hours later
After suddenly becoming available
"I could perhaps arrange it"

Perhaps

I know how busy her schedule is
I know how few windows she has open
I do not want to miss even one

And yet it is an issue of mine that I must face eventually

But now?
I don't know if I can
I don't know if I am strong enough
To miss seeing her because I am working
Because I am tired
Because I am sick
Because I am writing or needed somewhere else

I love her more than I have ever loved anyone
The need and attachment are not easily shed either

Another challenge is looming
I can feel it

When all I want to do is relax in her arms
Am I going to have to see her less to learn this one?

I hope not

When she wavers I tell her about the promise of The Path
That we begin to work off our karma
That life gets more challenging and
More rewarding
That we each create our situations
To learn the specific lessons in front of us
The quicker we learn them
The sooner our next step

Looks like I get to face my own preaching and
Hopefully the truth behind it
Not any more anxious to do so than Ari

FEELINGS AND FAILURES

I awoke from a nightmare before dawn
Cannot remember the last time I felt such terror
My sister told me at the beginning of the dream
That they had arrived in our city
And were being kept at a warehouse on the other side of town
She and I were scheduled to be picked-up
Dismembered and put back together again
In a gruesome parody of ourselves

We had to flee to live
As the dream ended we were packing
About to face our father with the news that we were leaving
Something which would hurt him tremendously
Unable to tell him we would be killed or worse
If we remained behind

Dealing with him while trying to survive seemed impossible

As the dream faded I awoke into a bloody pool of emotion
My feelings and failures with Ari swirling around my heart
Awakening too early
Swamped in depression
Needing more sleep
I lay in bed dozing until nearly nine
Feeling like there was nowhere to go
In my relationship with her
But down

Squeezed into a winless situation
As long as she is with Robert
As long as I loved her

I wondered when she would call me next
Would I say
"I can't break free right now
  How about in a couple of hours?"

I wondered what I would feel
If I jumped and ran as I have been doing
Always eager to make time to see her
Would she resent me?
Or worse—disrespect me?
And could she reschedule if I said I could not come now?

Monday morning and not a bit of fun on the horizon
The smiling pictures of Ari in Paris
Bringing up feelings of being mocked
Not joy

WHERE DO YOU WANT TO GO?

The day dragged on
A sack of cement around my ankles
Tripping me up
Sucking the moisture from my heart

I went home in the late afternoon for a nap
Could not sleep
Returned to work to meet my first telephone surveyor
After a too-long orientation meeting
And just as he was ready to begin calling
Ari called sounding cheerful

The key she set out for Robin the night before
Placed carefully in the derelict washer inside the gate
So Robin could clean the house on her schedule
Was gone
Stolen

I offered to replace the lock tomorrow
Ari said they weren't comfortable leaving the house
Unprotected overnight
So we began another handyman adventure

She wondered if she should come by now to pick me up
I said "No
  But I can be available in two hours maybe less"
I actually said it
I had no choice
The new telephone canvasser was there
Dependent upon my direction

And she adjusted her schedule to pick me up at nine

She was not as cheerful when I got in the car
Her day of depression seeping back over her
We went to my apartment so I could change clothes

But talked for an hour
About her feelings of disappointment
Anger
Frustration
Sadness
At me at Robert at herself at the situation

We compared our viewpoints on last night
She still very let down that
I could not support her need to go home to Robert
Because he was left alone and hurting
I could not let go of my hurt
Knowing that she would run home to him
After he had experienced nine hours of what I go through
Day after day

We reached out with our hearts to see the other's viewpoint
Even if we could not feel them

I shared with her my issue about personal space
Shared my hurt that she would think less of me for
Making myself so available to her
When I could do nothing else to be with her
In our situation

She told me I was wrong
I had misunderstood
She was concerned about my work
Concerned that I was neglecting my business to be with her
Taking it as a personal criticism when it was not
"I am always grateful and happy when you can see me
Especially with my unpredictable schedule"

I felt foolish
My hurt and hard-edged heart melted
It was my issue only
Probably
Certainly misconstruing because of discomfort

That I am not taking good care of myself

Our mood lightened but only after time passed
Talking about feelings and fears
When our laughter finally came
We both reached for it with relief
And hurried to her house to replace the work
Then have our elusive dinner of Korean food

Robin and her husband were still working
Determined to finish the cleaning that night
The deadbolt confounded me
No obvious way to remove it from the door except force
Finally I resorted to force
Hoping the door would survive
A twenty-minute job took an hour and a half

The house now lockable and secure
We left for our late dinner
But could find no Korean restaurant open after midnight
Both hungry but neither picky
We went back to my apartment
Drank protein shakes
Talked quietly of our love
Lay in each other's arms on top of my futon
Then shed our clothes in record time
Slid between the sheets for a few minutes of touching
Before she had to leave

We began making love as easily as we breathed
Then I felt her pull away
I asked her what she was going through
She said "I am so tired" and I knew she was

I felt like I was making love by myself so I stopped
Stopped too late
She was already sliding into her oblivion

She dressed in quiet distress
"I'm angry I can't do what I want to" she said
Her sadness smothered her anger I was sorry to see
Knowing she needed to let out
Whatever she is feeling

Before she pulled away
I leaned into the car and kissed her cheek
"I love you Beauty"
"Where is our love taking us?" she asked with eyes so sad
"Where do you want to go?"
She had no answer
Only sadness
I watched her car slip away into the night
Bracing myself to face the bed we had just left

PERHAPS AS ROBERT DID

Two quick visits with Ari today
One to take me to work in-between errands
After leaving my car at work the night before

The second to buy a wrap-around lock plate for the front door
To hide the bruises of the night before
I knew a wholesale house and needed to go in person

She picked me up from work
Looking down
Sounding sad

Robert had said little the night before
Was in bed but awake when she returned
Held her while she cried
Told her he loved her
Told her she was crying
Because she knew she was doing wrong

She told me of touching his cheek a few days earlier and
Asking him "Don't you like this?"
He said
"Sure I do
   Is he still grateful for your touch?"
"Why don't you ever hold my hand or touch me
   Except when we are in bed?
   Don't you need that?"
"No
   Not particularly"

"When we talk it is mostly about things" she said to me
"Mostly him talking"
She asked him why he always talked about
The endless details of life
Ignoring what to her had more meaning
Beginning with his feelings

"I tried that a couple of months ago
    But it did not work
    So why bother" she said he had said
Leaving the conversation at that

"I don't know what he's thinking about the situation"
She said to me
Sitting in the car after we had gotten the lock plate
"It's very unnerving
    I love him more for the understanding he is giving me now
    But I cannot talk to him
    Not about anything which has meaning to me today
    I feel so far apart from him
    Which is difficult
    But with the family
    I can't think of doing anything about it
    I don't know what to do"

I held her
Perhaps as Robert did the night before
Loving her
Trying my best to give her the space to grow
Succeeding today in my effort for the first time in too long

ODD JOBS

"I got a hug and a kiss from a woman at work today"
"Oh" Ari looked at me as she chewed her french fry
Always interested in the women I find attractive
And visa-versa
I knew I had her attention and paused, then said
"She's in her fifties
  We got her out of foreclosure"
"Good
  She got her money today then?"
"Not until next week
  She signed her papers yesterday and
  Stopped by with a couple of questions
  Wonderful person
  She hugged me the first time I met her
  So happy I was able to help her"

Ari squeezed my hand and took a bite of her hamburger
She on a fifteen-minute break from her store
Having to cover for the "responsible" worker
Who flaked out on Saturday

I was on my way to work
Having slept late and written for the rest of the morning
I was almost finding solid ground again
Making a very focused effort to be less burden to her
To choose lightness

She was better
But not fully healed from the past few days

We parted soon
Planning for me to return to her shop before closing
To fix her shelves and move two brass hooks
Before going to dinner and her new home

She called about six to tell me to come at

"Seven-thirty—no—forty-five"
I did not question her

I walked up to her store a few minutes early
Saw Robert standing inside
Hesitated
She saw me and waved me in

He was pleasant
Not offering his hand but accepting mine
"She has some work for you" he told me
"So I hear" I said biting back my humor
Not wanting to risk hitting a hot key of his

He left with a friendly wave
I felt very relieved and fixed her shelves
We talked and laughed
Actually had our Korean dinner together
Stopped by my office for fifteen minutes
To run off a flyer I had drawn for her
To send to the dance bars
"Slip it on: become a star
   Slip it off: become a sensation"
Some of Ari's imported clothes hot and sparkly enough
For show as well as play

Fifteen minutes became ninety
As we made love behind the couch
So close
So one

Dashing to her new house for more odd jobs
So I could put the metal plate around the deadbolt
Covering the scars from my earlier work
We discovered she only had the key to the side door

Laughing at ourselves
She put away bathroom things

While I repaired again the kitchen cabinet door hinge
Hanging out of alignment
Because I had re-hung it too soon after epoxying it

I drove us back to my car still parked near her store
She sleeping on the way
Asked her to call me the next day
Then kissed her good-night several times
As she slowly woke-up

UNFALLEN TEARS

Wondering if she would phone all day
I bought her seven thong panties tonight
For her birthday on Saturday
Their moving day when I probably wouldn't see her

She did call finally
After I had given up
Barely able to stay awake
Writing by feel

She told me the girls were coming home tomorrow
In LA tonight at her sister's
Freaked by too long a flight from Europe
Crying at not being with Mommy and Daddy for so long

She told me Robert had complained all day as they worked
They ran into an old friend at dinner and
Had a silly evening together

I managed to sit still
Feeling a stiletto run through me
Imagining her and Robert having fun together
And act which pushes me out of her world

"When might I see you next?" I asked
"I'll call you tomorrow early"
"When do you want me to finish your front door?"
"Anytime"
"Ten o'clock tomorrow night then"
"He was complaining about being with you almost every day"

With the kids coming back
With their long weekend of moving
It felt like I might not see her
For far far too long

She said she felt like crying
Feeling so pulled apart
Seeing Robert so sad

She said she missed me
I could hear it in her voice
Could hear her walking silently with her tears
Could feel my own tears
Held back by a whisper of effort
All that I have remaining tonight

Time for bed
Time to float into sleep and the inner worlds
Float on my personal ocean of tears
Slowly learning to navigate without being swamped
Without having to bail

RUNNING ON EMPTY

She did not call early
She did not call at all yesterday as she said she would

I wanted to curl up and yell
I wanted to hold her

I worked instead
Wrote in the morning
Worked at the office later
Dealing with a troublesome client
Helping a sweet one
Working with Bob on marketing strategies

Trying to understand myself
Listening to his advice about how to deal with Margie
Our excellent but problematic underwriter
She was having a good day
So I put off my talk with her
Letting my thoughts and feelings settle

Wondering if Ari would call
Wondering how many days would go by without seeing her

Did my taxes in a flurry in the evening
Not expecting to complete them until today
The fifteenth
IRS extension deadline
Ari's birthday

Went to bed late and sad
Putting one foot in front of the other
Seeing clearly my personal sea of emotion
Watching as I worked to relax
So I could float
My buoyancy providing safety as I feel what I fear
Instead of flailing hard to escape what I have created

Escape the pain
By doing anything
By trying to take myself anywhere else
Into blame
Into anger
Into lust
Into illusion
Drowning in my own wake

Found a familiar peace
Distantly familiar
When I surrendered my efforts to escape
Relaxing my gut
Trying to release the sprung steel coiled tight
From so many years of clinging dearly to my anxiety
That I might hurt
Holding the grief to me
Insuring my pain in a quixotic irony
From which I yearn to free myself

Ari called this morning
As I was resting after another unsettling phone call
With my grace-maker client of the moment
She not willing to see her situation
Her behavior
As I did looking at her as I know lenders would
Accusing me of being insensitive
Of being unkind toward women
She suffering from my desire to help
Someone out of foreclosure
To whom I would not loan my money if I had any to loan

Ari's voice on the phone soothed me
She in the heart of their move
The girls back earlier than expected yesterday
Unable to call
Because the phone was not hooked-up at the new house

Telling me this is the saddest Happy Birthday
Of her life
Telling me of crying in Robert's arms this morning
Him telling her she should not be crying
"You have two lovers
   No
   A husband and a lover
   Two great kids
   A new shop
   What more could you ask for
   You have everything" she told me he said
Then she said to me "He doesn't understand me"

"How can he" I thought
"He hasn't begun to face himself as you are doing"
But I did not say anything
Listening
She asked me how I was
I told her I was doing the best I could
Running on empty

"Get your move done Beauty
   I miss you terribly
   I'm working hard to not be angry
   To not blame you
   I'm sitting with my shit
   And I miss you as I miss my breath"

"You sound like a saint
   I love you"

Then she was gone
I had taken a small step
Not giving in to the awful pull in my gut

I thought of Robert's words
How he first termed himself her lover
Then changed to husband

The opposite of my terminology
Three days ago
When I felt hollow calling myself her other husband

Funny how both he and I want to be what the other is

FOREVER

On the phone with a realtor
Heard a scratch at the door then a knock
Opened it still listening to the agent go on and on

Ari!
Standing outside
The first time she had shown up without calling

Held Ari as the realtor continued her stories
Looking into Ari's eyes barely believing she was there
Finally said into the phone
"A friend just arrived whose birthday it is today
  How about I call you next week"

Then we were rolling on my futon kissing
Hugging feeling one again
Feeling myself being refueled with her love

I gave her the present
She read the card "Forever"
"Is this your name or mine?" she asked with a chuckle
"The next time we have a child we'll name it Forever"

She shook the box
"What kind of mischief do you have for me"
I just smiled and watched as she unwrapped it

The colors of the panties jumped through the tissue paper
Ari cooed with pleasure
"I like the colors" as she touched each one
Three whites plus blue lavender teal and rose
All thongs

"Where should I wear these?"
"The first place I want you to wear them is here for me"
She held up one of the white ones

"Is this the front?"
"Fine with me" I said
Then she turned it over and said
"No!
   That's the back you turkey"

We agreed she should wait until the move was over
To take them home

I asked her if we could plan an evening out each week or so
Since Robert had officially recognized my place in her life
"We had arguments the last two days
   About me spending too much time with you"

I told her I did not want to press her
Wanted to support her as much as possible
To handle my own stuff without it slopping onto her
Then said how much I was looking forward to next Saturday
When she had promised to celebrate her birthday with me

"There is an engagement that night
   Can we make it another time?
   I'm sorry"

I quickly got an opportunity to live up to my words as
My gut yelled at the loss

"How about Sunday" she said but added
"Let me check the calendar first"

Then she was gone after more kisses
Walking her to her car
Telling her I'd love her forever
Both of us grinning and waving as she drove away
Her words "I love you forever too" echoing in my heart

AT HER LIMIT

I stayed home from Sunday Service to write
Enjoying the rainy morning
By afternoon I had run out of energy
Tried to nap
Thought about going to the beach
Unable to focus
Surprised I was feeling unsettled so soon after seeing Ari
So soon after such closeness
Surprised and disappointed

By evening I was heavy into internal dialogue
Feeling the kick of my pain
Unable or unwilling to sort through the upheaval
Forgetting to notice the red flag of displacement
Thought after thought beginning with "She" and
Ending with reasons why my hurt was her fault

I went to bed in torment
"Didn't she love me?"
And awoke the next morning with the same fixation
By mid-afternoon I could not work
I stared out the office window
Wanting to cry
Not wanting to leave because she might call

Becoming desperate I called her shop
Gudren answered
Telling me Ari would be there at four-thirty
To stay at the shop until closing
While Gudren took Sarah to her Piano lesson

If Ari dropped Sar at her lessen
She could come see me for an hour
Why wasn't she planning this?
Surely Gudren could work longer
She would be waiting for Sarah anyway

My mind raced on
Rat-milling itself into a frenzy
I came home and cried
Felt lost
Bob called with a question about a loan and
I returned to the office to follow-up

Soon after I walked in Ari called from home to tell me
She would be at the shop from five to eight
Would I like to come down?

Locked in pain
Wanting much more
Than to stand around her shop for three hours
When I could not hold her
Kiss her
Or talk freely with her
I pushed away gratitude

I asked why she couldn't take Sarah to the piano lesson
She said she had left Gudren down there too long
Uncomfortable she had no work visa
"But you could come to see me" I said whining
"Yes I know" her voice went soft with regret
"Gudren also has to pick up a bicycle before five"

Case closed I shifted targets
"Can you spend some time with me after the store closes"
She hesitated then said "A little yes"
A little was not enough for my screaming kid and me

"I have a client coming at 6:00
   I'll come down after that" I said anger rising
"Oh"
She sounded disappointed

My client called at 5:30 to postpone our meeting

I walked into Ari's store twenty minutes later
Glum
Sad
Down
Firmly attached to my shit

She was smiling and bouncy
Hugged me
Kissed me gently
Made me sit down in front of the mirror
Standing behind me grinning she played with my cheeks
Kidding me about being unhappy

"Repeat after me
 I am Soul"
"I am Soul"
"I am Soul and I don't take 'No' for an answer"
"I am Soul and all I get is 'No' for an answer"
She laughed warmly but it didn't faze me
"I am Soul and I am happy" she said
"I am an unhappy Soul"
"You're hopeless" her smile beaming back at me in the mirror
Her hands stroking my cheek
I could not look at her for long
I could not look at myself at all
"I'm hopeless and miserable"

I held my sadness a little longer
Then began accusing her
"I'm getting buried under the mountain of things and people
 More important to you than me"
"I know" she said ruffling my hair
Sadness in her voice

"You could have called me yesterday
 You have a car and two legs
 You could have run an errand
 You could have taken an hour off to come see me"

"I had so much to do"

"You always have so much to do
   You always find something to do besides see me"

"I have to take care of my family"

"So who am I
   Some schmuck off the street
   I'm the guy you say you're in love with
   This relationship can die from lack of attention you know"

She lost her good humor
Turning inward to her pain which I had not thought about
"Maybe that would be better" her voice was quiet
"Fine" I said and stormed out of the store
I made it about ten paces
Then turned around and returned
Walking up to her
As she sat behind a display case mending a bustier
"Do you have any idea how I feel about you?"
I almost yelled my face inches from hers
She looked me hard in the eye and said
"Do you have any idea what I've been going through?
   Do you care about my feelings at all?
   Robert has been horrible all weekend
   So stressed out with the move
   His normal complaining self has turned unbearable
   He criticizes me the kids Gudren
   All day every day
   I am constantly reminding him to relax
   To stop complaining
   Nothing helps
   I would like to just disappear"

I felt like shit on top of shit
My heart was still closed

My two-year-old was still pounding on my guts
And I knew I had been very unfair

I sat down again and said
"You're right
    I'm sorry
    I haven't considered you"

I said it and I knew it but I did not feel it
It was hard for me to feel compassionate
For her trouble with Robert
Thinking she could be with me anytime she wanted

We talked in quiet tones
Both hurt and turned inward
I tried to draw her out when our feelings lightened
But I was too stuck to lead

Sadness covered us
Customers left soon after they entered the store
Closing time came finding us civil
Having left the arguing behind
Our hearts still closed
Love and Spirit shut out
Both miserable at the loss of our treasured closeness
I felt trapped by my own snapping dogs
Turning back on me after inciting them to attack
To find blame somewhere else
To make Ari the cause of my hurt

I went outside while she closed up
Heard a loud crash and came back in
She had dropped the change box
I helped her pick up all the coins
Then began counting them
Suggesting she take most of the silver and pennies home
Her change right for a candy stop
Not a specialty store whose sales averaged over fifty dollars

She agreed

We left later
Quiet
Walked to her car and got in like we knew where we were going
She buckled her seat belt then said "Are you hungry?"
"No but I'll come with you
   Or do you want to come to my place?"
"Let's go to your apartment
   I'll starve" she said
We debated picking up food on the way or me cooking
The take-out restaurants we thought of were closing
She didn't want any instant soup
She decided just to have a protein drink at my house and
Asked me to follow her over
Not wanting to return to the parking garage
After our time together
I wanted to ride with her but knew I could not object

I got out of the car then climbed right back in to kiss her
She responded more passionately than I expected
Our lips touching our hearts
Soothing the bruises left by our words

I climbed out again and walked upstairs to my car
Then drove madly down and out of the garage to catch her
She had not waited for me
My little boy screamed at being left
I ran two stop lights to catch her
Feeling stupid
Knowing I was risking getting a ticket
Perhaps then losing the whole evening with her
When I was behind her I did not honk
She did not wave

She parked in my stall
I parked on the street nearby
I was waiting for her when she got out

Wondering what I would do
With my little upset over her going ahead without me
"I thought you would wait" I said gently
"I did not" she was neutral
I said nothing else and
Followed her to my door and let her in

She dropped her purse in the kitchen and
Went to the bathroom without a word
Leaving a trail of tension behind her
Fumbling with my feelings
I made protein drinks and drank mine alone

She was sitting on the floor by my futon
When I brought her glass to her and sat it on a book
I plopped down on a big pillow against the wall
Looking at her profile
As she read a passage from one of The Path books
Tears welling

"You've had yours?" she said picking up her drink
"Yes"
She finished the drink
Turned a few more pages
Then came over to me

Her lips felt so tender as she kissed me
My hurt too fresh to let go of

My heart fell apart and I began crying
"It just hurts so much being away from you all the time"
"I know" she said and held me

My little boy was being given a chance to open for love
Warm loving arms held me
A sweet voice whispered in my ear
My adult saw what was a happening
Tried to coax my child to choose love

But left the reins in his hands

The downward momentum was too great
I—both child and adult—was too involved with pain
Sucking comfort from old familiarity
So attached to blaming her for my pain
"How can I trust her
....She left me!" my child screamed
Forty-year-old echoes of the nightmare
Waking to find my mother gone
Twenty-two months old
No Mommy
Then no Daddy
Then Daddy was back
Then he was gone again
My sister and me with Grandma and Grandaddy
"Where's Mommy and Daddy!"
No words able to reach me
No way to understand what was happening
My sister at nearly five
More aware that Mommy and Daddy were gone
Able to express her unhappiness in acts of defiance
I a sweet babbling two-year-old left with
A twenty-year time bomb set to explode repeatedly

"How do you think I feel every night
   Knowing you are curled up with another man?"
I sat up and pulled away from her
"It takes all my control to not think about you and Robert
   To not go nuts"
The old pain shook me
Tears of my abandoned two-year-old erupted
I cried harder than I had since
The night at the train station in Paris
The night Ari bowed to Robert's threats
The day we returned from Bali
The day of my father's funeral
The night alone with his body in its casket

"I can't stand to see you in such pain" Ari said
"I can't think or feel
   My heads feels like it's going to explode"

I heard her
The saw the sign that said she was at her limit
She often cannot handle my deep stuff
No reason to expect her to do so
I cannot
But I rushed on
Consumed with my grief
No compassion for her

"How could you settle
   For such an unsatisfying relationship?"
I listed all of Robert's faults I could remember

"I love him"
"But what kind of love?"
"I don't know
   The kids love their father"

"Kids love fathers who beat them too
   How far is it from emotional abuse to physical abuse?"
"He would never do that!"
"No I did not mean that
   I meant emotional abuse can damage just like hitting"

"I can't stand it" she said and buried her face in her arms
   Her words muffled
"I can't stand seeing Robert hurt so much
   I can't stand seeing you hurt so much
   I can't stand the pain anymore"

She looked up
She looked at me
She said in a clear cold voice

"I will never be able to see if my marriage works
  As long as you and are together
  Robert is confused
  I am so confused
  This is causing so much pain
  Maybe we need to stop seeing each other
  Maybe I should just go home and
  See if I can work out my marriage"

I went ballistic
"Oh great
  So now you are going to walkout
  It's great when you get what you want
  But when it gets rough you run home to Daddy"

"I'm going" she said and stood up
Angrier than I had ever seen her

I knew I could not face her leaving this way
I did not want her to run away
I knew we both would be miserable parting now
I took her wrist like we were shaking hands
And pulled her onto the futon in a gentle and firm motion
Which we have done to each other in play many times

I was careful
I did not want her to think I was getting violent with her
I have felt myself barely touch that line
Twice in the past
Touching no harder than I did now
But the feelings were communicated
The feelings of violence
Once when drunk long ago
Once when feeling very abandoned a few years later
Both acts costing me relationships
Lucky neither time did I hurt anyone
Lucky to learn that lesson without creating major karma

Ari was not frightened by me pulling her down on the bed
I put my arm around her and kissed her cheek
She stared at my bedspread

"I don't know how I could go on if you left" I said

She lay there tears dripping off the end of her nose
Then she rolled over, looked up at me and said
"I don't know how I could go on if Robert left me"

Her words did what cold water and slapping
Would not have done
They sobered me
This was Ari telling me how much her family meant to her
I saw it in her face
I saw it in her eyes
Her love for her kids
Her love for Robert
Her deep frustration with him
Her desperate desire to keep her family together

That she needed her family had not occurred to me
Beyond her desire for the kids to be with their father
Beyond what love she did or not feel for Robert
Beyond her cultural training
She—Ari—needed family
Why could I have not seen that in her earlier?

My heart softened
I could not keep pulling at her
Seeing so clearly she was doing what she needed

I could see her love for me
The joy and wonder it brought her
I saw how Spirit was using me and our love
To awaken her

I saw that I had work to do and

I was failing miserably at my job

I held her and kissed her hair
She began sobbing
"I don't feel love for anyone right now"

I rocked her whispering gently
"You can't feel anything
    When you keep your feelings trapped inside
    It blocks you up
    And it would be hard for anybody to stay open
    When they have two men hammering at them
    Especially two men you love and
    Don't want to choose between"

She bawled
It was wonderful to hear her cry
Knowing how important it was for her
Feeling her trust me
After all I put her through
How could I ever doubt her love for me?

I cried as she cried
Holding back my sobs not wanting to distract her
Our tears finally healed us enough to let Spirit in

In the next hour she said she was questioning
If there really was love between her and Robert
She said again how much it hurt her
Feeling Robert's pain
Behind each sarcastic crack he made about she and I
She said my pain hurt her so
She said her own pain was overwhelming her
She said she needed her family to stay together
She said she wanted to crawl in a hole and runaway

I opened still more to her and
Asked the Mahanta for help

Wondering why it had taken to so long to ask
A warm blue light poured through my heart and filled the room
My last pockets of darkness disappeared
She looked up at me and said without smiling
"You really are a turkey"
What could have ignited more harsh words earlier
Now brought laughter

Our last barrier burst
We made love tenderly
Surprising me
I did not think we would be able be this close
So soon after such a bloody time

Before she left she told me how much I gave her
How much she learned from me
I told her she gave me more in a smile
Than I had ever received from anyone else

As she was fixing her hair
She said
"I knew you and I were going to have an emotional day today"
"How did you know that?"
She smiled her silent smile and I asked again
"I know the more you miss me the more shit you give me"

She left with a series of passionate kisses

"I love you" I said
As I leaned through the window of her car
We both had exchanged those magic words
More than once in the last hour
She said "good-night" only
I knew she was still very troubled and
Tried not to let it hurt me

She heals more slowly than I
Because perhaps I heal by hurting her

I DON'T KNOW

I awoke this morning feeling dead inside
The aftermath of last night as tangible as
Garbage smeared all over my white carpet
Having pulled so hard at her
I now feared the repercussions and
Seeing ahead more clearly
What waits for me seems impossible

I know I must give Ari her freedom
But then how do I live?
If I hold onto her we will suffer greatly
Our love will suffer
Our growth
Her growth
My growth

Laureen has had to face this with her husband and children
Like many tests she often has to re-win it

Where do I go from here?
How do I find the strength to let her go?
How do I survive if she just goes?

I don't know

UNDERSTANDING

I stumbled through the day
Catching myself before anyone noticed at work
Taking a series of slow steps up a gradual ascent
Feeling like walking death yet determined
To pull out of the near-disaster of the night before
The possibility lingered Ari would surface
Having decided to break off our relationship

I didn't think she would do this
But who was I to predict?

I came home in the evening
Almost napped
Called Joe then Laureen
Neither were home

Began writing
As I watched the words flow across the screen
I felt my heart unravel
The knot of grief relaxed

The phone rang
Joe said "Hello from the east coast"
I listened to his story of near romance
Then told him about the previous evening with Ari
Surprised at my detachment

I heard a knock at my door and
Opened it still holding the phone
Ari stood outside
Sparkling in jeans and a green beaded bustier from her shop

I barely said goodbye to Joe
Then she was in my arms
So close
Our hearts pouring out to each other

"I came in then went out again
  I thought you had company" she said laughing
Her breath sweet an unusual smell surrounding her

As I held her I saw so clearly the path to her heart
We kissed and hugged
She told me how much she loved me
We kissed again
Lovers making up after a terrible evening of tears

"How are things at home?"
"They're all right" she said and
I felt relieved knowing
She had not gone home to another crisis

"I learned something last night" I said to her
Our lips inches apart
"What's that?"
"I learned about your need for your family
  Not culture
  Not duty
  Not hanging on so the kids are with their Daddy
  But Ari's need for family
  For your family"

She squeezed me hard laying her head on my chest
I stroked her hair
"I can only respect your needs
  Knowing this about you takes the wind out of my little mind
  As it accuses you of betraying your heart
  By following an old consciousness
  By not being with me
  I understand now you really need this
  And I will work as hard as I can
  To provide you the love and support you need"

"I'll understand if you ever need to stop being lovers

To work out your marriage
I'm sure I'll raise hell
But I'll understand"

The words flowed out of me as though dictated from afar
I knew I spoke what was in my heart
I also knew it was easier to talk of future possibilities
With her in my arms

She held me silently then pulled her head away from my chest
Looking away toward the corner

"Have I said something to bring you down?"
She looked at me her eyes afire with love
"I am so moved by your understanding"
"I can't promise I'll always keep it
I wish I could"
"I know" she said "But we learn each time"

I told her I had the insurance figured out
I would be seeing Rich beginning in two weeks
If it worked on her end
She said she saw no problem
Adding me to their company insurance
"I really want to get rid of this old baggage of mine"
I told her

We lay in each other arms
Holding
Kissing
Touching
She smelled like a freshly washed baby's bottom
Without the artificial smell of powder
"What's this incredible smell all over you?"
"Must be the soap" she said
"What kind"
"An Ayurvedic soap I found recently"
"Use it some more

I always love the way you smell
Just you no chemicals
But this is great too"

Then she was gone

She to her family
I back to my writing
Grateful for the gift from Spirit
The gift of love

YES

She called tonight before she came over
Having closed the store after Gudren worked
Filling in for whoever was scheduled and could not make it

When she walked in she seemed down

"Are you OK?" I asked
"Yes"
"Sure?"
"Maybe"

After I assured her I was doing pretty well she opened up
"Robert's as confused as I am
  In one of our many little comments back and forth
  He said today he just might give me my freedom
  That tells me how much he is hurting
  It's not the first time he has said it"

I held her and felt her tears begin
She sobbed into my shirt
"I'm afraid I'm losing him
  I really missed you last night
  I feel so close to you
  Your understanding means so much to me
  I've felt some of this for Robert when he's understanding
  But he doesn't hug me the way you do"

"Did he ever"
"No
  And he doesn't kiss me like you do either"
"He didn't used to kiss you at all"
"He doesn't know how"

She cried some more then evened out
We talked about Friday night class
She told me she had to work at the store

"Then I'll share class with you at the store"
"No
  You go to class
  I think some women are reluctant
  To try on things when you're there"
"So I shouldn't come by at all" my gut twitched
"You can come by for dinner" she smiled her smile of Beauty
"Sounds like you've found something else
  To come between us" my little boy whined
"I know
  I hated to say it"

I grumped a little more then let it go
Soothing my kid and staying open to her
Staying open to Spirit

A short time later I walked her down to her car
Kissing her through the open car-door window
I touched her cheeks and said
"I love you Beauty"
"I love you too Turkey
  I sure was brave last night
  To even mention not seeing each other
  You might have taken me up on it"

I grinned
"Yes you were brave
  And I love you for your bravery"

I waved to her a last time as she drove away
Then stood on the sidewalk after she was out of sight
Reminding myself she and Robert
Go through many ups and downs
Trying to detach from any hope her news might give me

I asked myself if I wanted her enough to heal my two year old
To let go of my closely guarded grief
Did I want her enough

To give her support and love
To give her the freedom to make her choices
No matter how awful it felt
No matter how much work it took

"Yes
  Yes
  Yes I do"
I chanted to myself
As I took the stairs up to my apartment two at a time

"Yes
  Yes
  Yes I do"

Now I just needed to find a way to do so

HUSH

"There are times when I wish I was all yours
   Like now"

We sat in her car on an empty street in Kakaako
Parked between an abandoned car and two run-down trucks
The metamorphosizing warehouse district of Honolulu
Lay around us
Construction lot on one side covered in weeds and dirt mounds
Enduring the slow process of soil decontamination
Twin forty story towers a block behind us shining and new
The block closest to us on our right derelict
Two large trees standing alone guarding rubbish
A low concrete block building forlorn beyond the trees

"There are times when our hearts melt together stopping time"
I had just said to her
Just put into words a new clarity about mothering

"Remember when I snapped at you not to mother me"
She smiled and nodded
"Well I found out tonight in class
   Just one of those flashes that pop up
   That more than anything"
I paused then said
"This is hard to say but
   I really do want your mothering
   Just the way I want to care for you
   I would love to be mothered by you
   It is so hard though because the little boy in me
   Who craves this
   Who missed it as a child
   Is the same little guy
   Who goes nuts when you leave
   Especially when he opens up enough
   To accept some mothering from you
   It's a tough one, Beauty

I hope I can work through it with Rich
 When I start seeing him"

She stroked my cheek
We sat in the front seat
The cassette storage console
preventing us from touching below our shoulders
"Have you made an appointment with him"
"Yes
 Wednesday after next—the second"
"I hope it goes well " she said then kissed me
Then said with such tenderness
"There are times when I wish I was all yours
 Like now"
My heart wanted to soar but I calmed it
Keeping the awareness so recently and painful won
That Ari is doing what she needs to be doing for herself
She wants and needs to be with her family

I kissed her and ran one hand down over her arm and breast
Her breath caught
Such a wonderful moment to have begun a night together upon
"If that is ever to happen
 It will be a wondrous time"

"Hush" she said putting her fingers to my mouth
We kissed again
Then she said "I'd better go"
Five minutes later we were in separate cars
Waving goodbye
As I veered right off South street onto King and
She went straight heading for the highway

HAPPY BIRTHDAY

I said good-bye to Janet Kealoha
An articulate woman in her fifties who had buried her head
After she helped her oldest son rather than pay her mortgage
And now was weeks away from losing her home
Having neglected to open the mail for months
Except for my marketing letter

We had just agreed on the use of funds for a rescue loan
From a private investor who had given loan approval
The day before without seeing any paperwork
A rare and lucky accomplishment
We planned to begin processing a new first mortgage
To pay off the investor after his loan funded

A complex arrangement of business details
Structured to meet Mrs. Kealoha's needs in a reasonable way
Give the investor enough return to warrant his risk and
Satisfy three attorneys
Her existing lender and her foreclosing association

The meeting took longer than I expected and
I reached for the phone to call Ari
On the chance she was still at her shop
Ninety minutes after she planned to leave

The phone rang before I touched the receiver
"Hi
   Still working?" she said in her soft almost lilting voice
"I just finished this moment"

We met at Ala Moana and
Spent the next hour racing through women's clothing shops
Talking on the run
Looking at labels and prices
She occasionally trying on something
One store offered me the "husband chair" while I waited

Our last fifteen minutes together
We parked in the lowest level to share tenderness
I waved goodbye to her bouncing with energy
Feeling like I could handle the evening alone writing

The next morning she was five minutes late for Sunday Service
Scolded me for waiting for her
We dashed up to the Center
Without taking the full moment I needed to link up our hearts

My little boy whined throughout the Service
I tried to soothe him
To convince him it wasn't worth fretting about
Afterward we left for a quick hour together
Before she needed to pick-up a friend's daughter

I mentioned my small dilemma
We talked it through in a small way
Acknowledging our differences
She soothing me with her love

We played on the grass at the University for minutes
I teased her I had devised a new way of pampering her
Then she was gone
Planning to come back that evening to celebrate her Birthday
A week-late date agreed to by Robert

She came at seven grinning
Jumped into my arms
I sang Happy Birthday to her three times
She endured my voice with grace

"Want's your curfew tonight?" I asked her
Holding my breath afraid to hear 10:00 or 11:00
"I asked Robert when should I be home
   And he said 'Why don't you sleepover'"
"And you said...?"

"When the children saw I was going out
    They pleaded with me to be home early
    I told them I would be back about midnight"

Midnight
Not too bad
I relaxed

"The children were all over me when I left
    Telling me how much they loved me
    I told them individually 'I love you' and
    Said the same to Robert
    He said 'Mommy loves everybody'"

We both laughed at Robert's joke
"That's really funny" I said amazed
Wondering where he really was about the situation

I was over-charged for our evening together
Wanting to squeeze a lifetime of yearning into
Our few hours together

We debated about eating
Before seeing the new Meryl Streep - Goldie Hawn movie
She wanted to see
Ari loves Meryl Streep

Then we ran out of time for dinner
Ari thought of ordering now and picking up after the movie
I called
Finding a Thai restaurant open late enough and ordered

She wanted to try on her birthday panties
Opened on her birthday eight days earlier
But left with me for now
Seven pairs of thongs
I warned her we would be late for the movie
If she took off her pants

She grinned and said
"Let's wait for that
  Help me off with these
  Pick out which pair
  You want me to wear"

I got the white lace ones and put them on her backwards
"Hey they don't go on that way"
"But they look so great in front" I said then
Teased her with my tongue
When I licked around to her bottom I said
"Your right they're saggy in back"

We put them on the right way and found they were too big
The rose pair was smaller than the rest
So she slid her jeans up over them and
We rushed off to our movie
Which was so dumb we both wanted to leave in the middle
But neither mentioned our boredom to the other
So we stayed until the end
Yawning and feeling very tired as we left

We picked up the Thai food
Stopped by her shop to get last night's receipts
Then went home for a candlelight feast of
Bangkok Wings
Spring Rolls
Curry
Garlic Vegetables
Talk of the next Bali trip
Each other

She giggled when I told her of my plans for
Fun with the rowing machine
But we decided to postpone that adventure
Our time and our energy limited

Our lovemaking was soft and warm
I licked her from her nipples to her knees
Settling about halfway in between
Bringing her to the moment of orgasm again and again
But never quite there

She pulled me up to her and said
"I don't know if I can tonight
  You bring me so close
  Then Robert's face haunts me
  Seeing him at home knowing what we are doing
  Holds me back"

Her reaction was plausible in our situation
And not unreasonable
But it gutted me
I lay on top of her one arm holding most of my weight
Feeling my life-force drain away

She told me how much his efforts to give her understanding
Pulled at her
How frustrated she felt
Not being able to be completely with me

I grew numb inside

"Do you want me to leave" she asked
"I never want you to leave"

Slowly I moved through long moments of lifelessness
I felt the impulses flash to blame her
Some how I was able to let it pass by
Knowing I did not want to hurt her
Knowing she was being open with me
Following my pledge to support her in her feelings
No matter what she felt

She asked me what I was feeling and I told her

Then she said
"I get so confused
  I just don't know what to do"

From inside of me I heard myself say
"Follow your heart and open more each day to Spirit"
"Follow my heart?"
"Yes"
"My heart tells me to love you
  And to have a wonderful family"
"Then that's all you can know right now
  Do it the best you can
  Just as Robert and I struggle to give you your freedom
  Each in our own way
  You will have to free yourself of your attachments
  Eventually
  To everything and everyone
  There are steps along each of our paths
  Which require letting go
  If we are to go on
  No telling when you or I or Robert
  Will come to one of those steps"

"Being on The Path increases the chances of
  Finding those steps in this lifetime"

We melted into each other
Spirit washing away our pain
Opening our hearts farther as we made love

When she had to go
When she was dressed and in my arms
She kissed me deeply
Hugged me and said
"I am so glad you are mine
  Are you?"

"Without doubt or hesitation

I am yours"

Then we held each other so tightly
Trying to keep it forever

She looked around before we walked out
"Is this all I have?
Isn't there something else I should take with me?
The bed?
You?
The rowing machine?"
I laughed "Take whatever you can carry"

"I couldn't ask for any more than I have right now"
Ari said holding me tightly
"You couldn't handle anymore either" I whispered

She squeezed me again then pulled back and looked at me
"Being in two beds in one night is very hard for me
For you too I imagine"
"The only thing hard for me is being away from you"

We went through our parting ritual
Hugging in the elevator during its one-floor descent
The shock of physically separating as she got into her car
Kissing her through her open window
Walking slowly in front then beside her
As she pulled up to the driveway
Kissing her again
Mutual "I love yous" murmured or not
Waving as I backed away from her car a final time
Watching as she eased onto the busy street
Then when she could look back as she drove away
A last wave
Sometimes from the sidewalk
Sometimes from the first-floor landing
Always walking back into my apartment flooded with feelings
Usually conflicting

As I closed my door on our evening together
I wondered how long before
We could spend another few hours as lovers
The immediate future did not look bright
Yet I did not feel the sharp loss

Was I handling my little boy better?
Had I made a shift?
Or was it only momentary?

I surprised myself by feeling the place up ahead
Where my need runs out and my little boy panics
Not realizing he has let go of the old hurt

In the past he and I have reached instinctively
For familiarity
Pushing away whatever relationship is no longer feeding us
Running from the chance to step into a new level of love

I made a note to stay on top of this old dynamic
If it happened and
I wondered if Rich was already at work on the inner
Then knew he was

NEEDING REASSURANCE

Ari called about 5:00 at work the next day
Talking about a possible itinerary for the Bali trip
I had been even all day
But now felt myself sliding into mud puddles

I wanted desperately to go to Bali with her again
Late October would be about right with the office and
My cash flow
But her need for inventory
Was threatening to move up our timetable

I felt fear
Fear that I was pushing myself into a financial trap
Afraid of letting her go without me
Afraid I would botch my credit and
Lose my travel freedom

I was still numb from the night before
When our lovemaking was stopped in mid-stride
By her confession that she was seeing Robert
Feeling badly he knew we were together
Focusing on this troublesome moment
Instead of when we opened more fully to our love

"I'm okay in my heart with Robert
   I'm okay in my heart with you
   I have trouble when I put you both together"
She said on the phone as I sat in my office

I ask her how she would be with Robert alone
"We'd surely be more open
   If I wasn't seeing you
   We tip-toe around each other now
   Being so careful"

"How would it be with just me"

"We could build a much deeper and broader relationship
No I'm not sure we could get deeper
I've never been this deep before
I'm sure we could expand our foundation though"

I was trying to make her look at being without me
"I can understand how you and Robert would relax
Without the tension of our situation
But how would you be
Without you and I to feed yourself"

"You know how I would be
That hasn't changed"

"Sometimes it's nice to say it again
What is obvious to you
May not be obvious to someone else"

"I'm not ready to bind myself to Robert forever
I don't know where his consciousness is going
I know I don't want to live the rest of my life
With him as he is today
I don't want to live the rest of my life
With myself as I am today"

I warmed hearing her commitment to growth
She continued
"I would be so empty without you in my life too
You know that"
I sighed
That was the issue
She was consistent in her love and her efforts to be together
But I keep forgetting
Keep needing to be reassured

My telephone surveyors arrived and we had to hang up
Good thing
I was still unsettled and

About to pull at her some more

When I got home the apartment was full of flowers
Roses on the table
Roses on my desk
In the bathroom
The special big white roses Ari brought me in May

I knew enough about her schedule that day
To know she had left them before we talked

WHY'S THAT?

"If you ever get serious about me
   Michael is one of a handful of people you can ask
   About how crazy I used to be"

"Why would I ask someone else
   Why not just ask you?"

"They might give you a different perspective"
I said to Ari having fun

"Maybe I'll ask him when I meet him Sunday"
"That's a good sign"
"Just in case I ever get serious about you"
"Oh"
"Maybe what he says will prevent that happening"

"It's a good thing then you live with Robert and not me "
"Why's that?"
"If we lived together
   How would I ever get Michael alone
   To coach him on what to tell you"

"If I lived with you
   I'd already be serious about you
   So it wouldn't matter what Michael said"
"You might change your mind
   Yes Ma'am, I'd better talk to him"

We were on our way to Liberty House
To exchange her Birthday Panties and
To buy something for Sarah's Birthday tomorrow

"Just what is it you want to hide from me?"
"Only my true character and my past, Beauty
   Nothing else"
I grinned and squeezed her hand enjoying our play

We were on our eleventh day since our last fight
The big one, two Mondays ago
I was working every minute to ride-out my internal sunspots
Flashing without apparent justification
Leaving clues behind in the shadows and ashes
If I took the time to look

Earlier in the week
I had weathered my discomfort at Ari's reports
That life at home was peaceful
That Robert was understanding
Information which so easily panics my little boy
Fearing I would lose her

I watched him squirm this time
Soothed him
But did not give in to his demands and
Learned more about his triggers

The wave of energy which flows from me through Ari to Robert
And back from him through her to me
Had reversed its course again

Ari had been in my arms for an hour
Before we left my apartment to go shopping
Softly telling me of Robert's complaining
Of his worry over money
Of his crabby refusal to plan anything special
For Sarah tomorrow
Of his counting the minutes every time she ran errands
Telling her she was spending too much time with me

"Next time he says you're spending too much time with me
Tell him I have a completely different point of view"
"So do I!" she said
"Good news to me"

She was feeling the distance with her husband and
Holding me tightly
Our love flowing
Washing over her
Healing

"Why can't I just be happy no matter what's happening
Why do I choose to feel sad?"
Her words echoed in my apartment
I asked on the inner whether to answer or
Let her question slowly dissipate

I got an inner nudge to share my thoughts and
The awareness that her answers only come from within her

"We create our worlds
Yet change often comes slowly
On one of his recent tapes
Sri Thomas talks about a fellow who decides
He is going to increase his income ten-fold in a week
The guy is not willing to take small steps
Has not laid the groundwork
So he fails of course

"You have a certain amount of momentum
In your life
With Robert
With the girls
With the rest of your family
Changing that takes time and work

"It's great you now have the awareness
That your life is yours to create
But I don't know anyone who's always happy
While they have a physical body
I am happier the more I stay in touch with myself as Soul
It takes patience Beauty"

She sighed and hugged me
"When I was unpacking last week
  One of my old journals fell open
  It was from six years ago
  I wrote then that
  I had lived half my life and accomplished nothing
  That all Robert was doing was complaining and
  I was so tired of his shallow self-righteousness"

"Quite an indictment"
"I was pretty unhappy then too"

When together Ari and I seem to step lightly
On unseen softness
Time speeding ahead devouring our time together
This Friday was no different

The lingerie department at Liberty House
An unsuccessful tour of Girls 7- 14
Kisses in an empty elevator
The watch counter
Her threats to buy me a suit
"What on earth for?"
Hand holding in back aisles
Me telling her as we returned to my home
"Tell him you will not get tired of me
  If we don't spend enough time together"
Were all behind us in a moment
Three hours felt like three minutes
As I kissed her goodbye and
Watched her drive away
Surprised for the thousandth time
How the prospect of parting felt fine when with her
Yet so devastating as she left
Part of my heart ripped away
Grinning and waving
Always leaving
"But I always come back" she reminds me when I whine

"Come back soon Beauty
   I can't live too long without you" I said to the wind
Her car no longer in sight
Remembering how she giggled as I licked her legs
While she tried to put on her lipstick in the bathroom

HOPE SURGING

Arms and legs
Assholes and elbows
My world all akimbo these past ten days

Travel agenda for Bali set
Michael in town
Nearly panicking at work trying to cram a month into two weeks
Looking under rocks for money
To pay for the trip in advance
The travel agency not accepting plastic for these specials
Looking for cash to repay Ari
Her loan to me from eight months ago
So she would have enough cash for this buying trip
Worried about bills
My pipeline of loans drying up
Concerned about leaving Bob unsupported at the office
Again

Michael back home after asking him for a loan
Dropping him off at the airport
Only a few days after telling Ari I felt past the old urges
To visit the dance bars
My short visit to the Pigalle area in Paris my cure
Driving from the airport pulled by a wave of lust
My resistance succumbing
Because I had not maintained a good focus on Spirit
I spent a couple hours drenched in the intoxication of
Smiling women reeling me in with their slender bodies and
Artful manipulation of their sexual energy
Drawing from the Psychic Circus a currency
Understood by all in a physical body

They creating karma for themselves
I answering their call
By supplying the physical manifestation of
Their desired currency

Creating for myself a back-wash of lower vibrations
Straining my physical health
Popping anchoring points for my emotional body
Restimulating old causes
Feeding mental concerns
Violating the Law of Economy by using money carelessly
I crawled home accepting my choices
My inner bodies reverberating with the pounding of the bars

I did not tell Ari
Wanting to deal with my effects myself
Now wanting to make her my therapist this time
Not wanting to risk her rejection this time

The next two evenings with her a roller coaster inside
Working hard to support her
As I wallowed without anchor

Then she left for Los Angeles
A quick trip for her shop
Calling me at the airport as she boarded and
Again as she deplaned here three days later
Unable to call in between
Conversation with her sister peppered with
Discussion of Ari's "friend"

The girls had confessed to their Auntie
Earlier in the summer on their way to Europe
Of their distress over
"Mommy and Daddy fighting all the time"
Both wished BC was a woman
"So we wouldn't have to worry
 When he and Mommy are together
 Wouldn't have to worry they would get married"

"Will you marry him?" Ari's sister had asked her
"I don't know " Ari had then shared with her sister
The depth of feeling in our special friendship

But missing in her marriage
Yet she could not risk disclosing our intimacy

The Bank of Michael was able to grant my loan request
Enabling me to finish paying Ari and Robert for my ticket
Which they booked and paid for
And to repay Ari her from-out-of-nowhere save-my-ass loan
The day we became lovers

My first session with Rich anti-climatical
Dealing with addictive behavior and dreams
He showing me how a horrible dream the week before
Was a dream of warning of the upcoming hormonal tsunami
Wanting to work on hard issues always easier than the work

My body could not stand the additional stress
From the two hours in the dance bars and
I developed a terrible cold
Sobering me
Forcing me to rest

During Ari's absence I worked hard to heal my body's
Physical-Emotional-Causal-Mental
Arlean's Friday class on spiritual awareness helped a lot
Taking small steps I healed on the inside
Laughed and teased with Ari
When she called on Saturday
From the airport and from home
Her only two chances to call
No chances to come by

Sunday morning I crumbled on the way to Service
My little boy in pain ready for battle
She had not called to say she would make the early Service
She had not made time to see me in between

I waited for her near tears
Not wanting to fight but full of pain and recrimination

Sure she would be there at the last possible minute
Her recent pattern
That would give us no opportunity
To greet each other heart to heart before Service

She parked her car next to mine with ten minutes to spare
I told my little boy to let go of his harpoon
She got into my car when I did not get out
Bent to me
Kissed me on the cheek and asked me what was wrong
I told her how I felt
I told her my mind wanted to blame her
But my heart did not

She held me tightly
I felt myself open to her when I said "I love you"
She responded with those magic words and I melted
"I feel like the kid who falls and hurts his knee
    Walks home without a limp
    Then begins crying as soon as he sees his mother"

We laughed as I explained how clear I had stayed
About her being gone until twenty minutes before
"I should have been here twenty minutes earlier" she said

A month ago I would have ruined both our Sundays
It has now been three weeks since I have pulled at her to
Make me and my kid feel better

After the Service we raced to my apartment
I had an hour until a meeting back at the Center
She had Robert on her back to do things with the family

We undressed each other as we drank protein drinks for lunch
Then made love like we had been apart for months

"I missed you the most while I was gone"

She said at one point
I did not comment except to joke that
I missed her the most too
Later she said "You were the only one I missed"
I looked up into her eyes as she sat astride me
"What are you telling me Beauty?"
"I'm scared
   I love you some much it scares me"

My heart could not open any wider to her
I smiled and held her hand as she gently moved her hips
My hopes surging

HOPE DASHED

Then they were dashed
Barely thirty hours later
Thrown on the floor like dirty socks
My heart crumbling
My little boy crying out for love
My heart shut down unable to nurture

The high aspirations of the day before
Stinking like shit in the corner
As I reached out to her and found no support
As I shook her and was slapped away

A simple act of greed
Losing sight of gratitude
Letting pain rule

Now I sat in the backwash of my actions
Tears blurring these words
Her words stinging me anew
"I can squeeze you in for a few minutes tomorrow
Before my dinner Robert and our dinner appointment"
What I keep hearing

She was not able to come see me today
Sarah with a fever canceling her violin lesson
I did not fully expect to see Ari
I hoped and
When I heard her say she was at home unable to leave
My hopes crashed
I told her of my disappointment
I teased her to come out anyway
Ignored her when she said she was disappointed too
Her voice small and quiet

My anger seeing only she was choosing not to come see me
She was choosing not to tell me how much it hurt her

In words I could hear
She was laughing when I first answered
How could she be hurting?
What did she care?
She was with her family
She could not have her popsicle today
I would have to go without my oxygen

Down I went into self-pity and anger

She was not in good shape herself
Locking down after my first couple jabs

When I am full of unexpressed pain
I shut off to others
Especially others who pull at me
Her reaction was telling
I saw it later when I had calmed down
Too late to join hearts
Hers shut away for longer than the phone call would last

If she had opened the conversation
Expressing her sense of overload
Of telling me how much she looked forward to seeing me
Of how disappointed she was
I would have been different
I would have felt needed

When she laughed and said she couldn't come see me
When she was still light and gay after I opened to her
When she then told me she would "squeeze me in" tomorrow
I felt unneeded
Unloved
Taken for granted
Our two weeks in Bali only ten days ahead
Yet non-existent in the moment
As my child reached for reassurance
Reached past the meager company I offer him

Reached out to her and
Fell without her support
On his gentle blond-haired face

Then he came up screaming like a hideous monster
Kicking unmercifully at all around him

My control slipped
But not that badly
She turned cold so fast saying
"I know you were due
   I know you so well"
It felt like a slap

The past three weeks of working so hard to be there for her
Unrecognized
She spoke of Robert's pain about the upcoming Bali trip
Of her discomfort when she knows he knows
We are together for more than hour
The pain I live with
Knowing she is with him all day every day
Unrecognized

Just because I have a need does not mean she can fulfill it
I know this
Tonight it is hard to bear
Gratitude is less than a whisper

What am I working to build if she cannot see it
So locked into her family
So unable to be happy with just her family
Having what she says she wants

Robert wants her full time
Does not have it
I want her full time
Do not have it
She has her family

She has Robert
She has me

I know this is the little view
Yet tonight I cannot get past it
I cannot find my reservoir of patience for her
It is nights like this when words fly and worlds fall apart

I am glad I am alone
Unable to do more damage
There are many words she says
"Robert and I will never pull our marriage back together
   As long as I keep seeing you"
"My life would be so empty without you"
"I love you so much it scares me"
Words that I play again and again just to keep going

I should be happy just to wait
Working to not screw-up things if nothing else
But my fire-sign mouth
My urgent need to sooth my kid
My constant inner urging to press on
To push the envelope
To understand more
To express more
Keep ruffling the still pools around me
Keep upsetting Ari's life
Keep attracting her to me?
I so hope

AROUND THE CORNER AND ACROSS THE STREET

When I attack she pulls away
Then faced with the choice of losing her
Or continuing my anger
I reach out to Ari for much longer than I was angry

This time it required all my effort
Through a long, late-night call Monday
Only hours after I was so petulant
Massaging her with my heart and fingers on Tuesday
During our "lunch"
And again on Wednesday
During three hours of soothing

Such a tender young heart
Stung while venturing out
Still fresh and vulnerable
Shocked into retreat by the whiplash sting
Of her lover's tongue

Thursday morning I awoke sad
Feeling in touch with Ari
Past the momentary barrier of my own creation
Felt the previous two days
But still sad with my own pain unworked through

I sat in the chair in Rich's office
For my second session with him
Brushing off a few flakes of remaining disappointment
From our first appointment
Expectations raised beyond reason
By the moments shared as friends over the past four years

I asked if we could do a HU
He said he had thought of that a couple days before
But wanted to find out where I was before we did
So we could focus the inner work

Forty-five minutes later I told him

Told him about Ari and my anger
Told him about my sadness
Told him about the dream a few nights earlier
In which I was given a book
Showing my father in a straightjacket before he died
Shown this was what he had to do to himself
To be able to continue the last few weeks
Before holding my stepmother at gunpoint
Wanting her to repent her adultery
So he could send them both to heaven
With the help of his old hunting rifle
Before I drove three long hours to his house
Selected to defuse the situation
After my sister's call
I having the only keys to the house
Unable to reach him
I let him continue on his course
Twenty-four hours later he dropped his physical body
Leaving my step-mother to her own path

I awoke with the grief of his parting
With the grief of his life washing over me

I told Rich about my awareness of my just past lifetime
Gained over several months through various spiritual exercises
Showing me I was Charlie Reynolds
My father's best friend as a boy
Living around the corner and across the street

I shared with Rich how I was shown the experience
Of breaking through the clouds over the Mediterranean
In my fighter
Feeling the intense vibration of the plane
Going down and down surrounded by blue
Swallowed by blue

Trailing a white marker lingering over my grave
No longer than a whisper echoes

I had returned to Mt. Carmel without my physical body
To find Bill with my girl
Not having shed my emotional body yet
I was hurt and left sooner than needed

Another time at a Seminar of The Path
Seated between two women
One German
One French
During a HU with five thousand people
I heard my two friend's accents resonate and
Was overcome with World War II emotions
The love of a French woman
The fear and hatred of the Germans
The reason I was so far from home
Risking my life for what I did not know

"So you carry the guilt of not saving your father
   And your best friend" Rich said

His gentle validation opened me

Through the tears
I talked about my awareness as a very young boy
Sent to live with my father's parents
Send to live in the very house Dad grew-up in
Grew up as Billy
Send to live across the street and around the corner
From my home
From the house which had been my home eight years earlier

I felt the waves of loss roll over me
My best friend Bill
My Dad
My mother in this lifetime

My mother in my last lifetime
Where was she?
She who I had been so close to
She who I always patted her patootie
When leaving, saying
"Love you Mom"

Sitting in Rich's office I felt my connection with her
Surface suddenly
A surprise opening me more

Rich suggested we HU

I sang the tone low and long
The sound surrounded me and I
Felt myself reaching out to Robert
Wanting to help him
To show him how he creates his own prison
By holding onto his pain
In his effort to keep it away
Then I saw I could not reach him
Today he does not understand
Like my father who did not understand
Then tears erupted

When I got back to the HU
Rich guided me gently
Refocusing me on the Sound and Light
The inner manifestations of Spirit
Whenever I would veer off with my mind

Thoughts are used in a contemplation
To open the inner doorways
Unlike meditation where the goal is no thought

Rich continued to work with me as we sped along
Hearing the HU on the inner
"You are holding yourself at one tone" he said

"You keep from nourishing yourself
Try to let go
Try to go with the rhythms of Spirit"

I knew exactly what he was talking about
Like Robert I hold my pain to keep it away
While closing to the food of Spirit
Closing to Love

After the HU we talked about the similarities between
Robert
Ari
Zak
And of Robert and my father

Riding the elevator down to my car
I wondered if there was a connection between
Ari and my mother in my past life
My mind doubted
I felt no inner nudge either way so I let it go
Wondering what became of the woman who lived in the house
Around the corner and across the street

BEYOND REASON

How do I take another step?
How do I keep on?

Tears too many to count
Awake after forty minutes of sleep
My physical body still on Bali time
Thinking it is waking from a dinner-time nap

My emotional body warping
Twisted with pain
Knowing far too intimately the results of need run rampant
Leaving me weak
Too weak to be strong for Ari
Not strong enough to handle my feelings
As she gives herself to her family

After two weeks together in Bangkok and Bali
Two weeks of non-stop work
No time for relaxed play
No time to see the sights
Two weeks of market research negotiating buying
Two weeks of being at each other's side
I should be stoked for months

Instead I grew numb the last few days
Numb from feeding my need
Neglecting my spiritual exercises
Neglecting my rhythms
After opening so much to her
I was scared to be away from her
Afraid she would not come back

Beyond reason
Playing out for the countless time
My child's frozen fear of being left alone

Aware of my choices
Riding down the rollercoaster chute
Unable to choose a different track
Earning Ari's deepest gratitude
While risking emotional suicide
Growing too numb to make love
Without using images of other women to control my performance

On the plane ride back we sat a seat away Emma
One of her employees
A wild chance only Spirit could arrange
The last fifteen hours of cuddling with her taken away
Because Emma knew Robert
Knew Ari as a married woman
The plane too full to change seats

My little boy became furious
After harsh words and uncontrolled tears
I settled down feeling foolish
Grateful Ari forgave my weakness

On the ground in Honolulu through Customs behind her
Delayed by Spirit's hand
So she could be surprised by Robert without me standing there

When I emerged from the inspection area
She came up to me
Told me he was there
Her eyes telling of her happiness to see him
Cutting my heart to pieces
Too blind to see her love for me
Unable to look beneath her control
To see her tears which she dare not show me
For fear they would still be there when she walks to Robert

"I'll call you soon" she said
"Why bother"
My child petulant

My adult knowing to not leave in the hot moment
I whined my feelings
Carefully avoid words that would hurt her
Then after a long hug which reminded me of
Watching Robert hug her good-bye two weeks earlier
I tumbled into a cab as I had done five months before
Crying most of the way home

After paying the cab driver
I dragged my luggage into my apartment and
Collapsed into sobs
Wondering if I would ever be able to let go of my pain
To let Spirit in
To let Spirit heal me

TOO FAR ALREADY?

In my mailbox was a postcard from Ari
Written six days earlier
While we waited for the delayed flight
From Bangkok to Denpasar, Bali
Written while I pouted after seeing her write "Dear Robert"
On the first of four cards
Feeling insecure being so open
So defenseless against the coming separation

Written when only the name Mr. Lolo reached me
"Come on Mr. Lolo
   Show Mrs. Lolo how to play Backgammon" she had said
Taking me by the hand
"Or is your doodoo-filled brain too full
   To remember how to play?"
We had begun calling ourselves by the Hawaiian word for crazy
For being so lolo about each other
For being so silly
Laughing in near-constant child-like delight

Standing by my mailbox in Honolulu's warm September sun
I read
"Dearest Zak
   On your first visit to Bangkok
   Not able to make any leisure time
   Not able to go north with you
   To show you my old home in Chaing Mai
   Not able to hug you and kiss you when you need it
   I'm very sorry
   All the help you have extended to me selflessly
   I'm dumbfounded
   My heart opens to you all the way
   Sorry we are too much in public to express
   Still looking forward to spending every moment
   We have left together on this trip
   With open hearts filled with love

Forever yours
Ari"

I felt like a fool again
Remembering how I acted as she wrote those words

She called me at work two hours later to say
She was running errands after a short nap
We planned to meet at my apartment

I went to Laureen's for a Jin Shin Jyutsu treatment
To soothe my bodies
To help bring me home
To help heal

After the treatment Laureen told me
To wrap myself in the Golden Light of God
She told me I was standing at a doorway
Trying to push open a door that
I needed to let open by itself

I could feel the Light pouring through me
A sound like rustling leaves filled my head
Then grew into the steady roar of a strong wind

Laureen told me to fill myself with the Love of God
To bathe in Its White and Gold Light
To feel the pain
That growth comes with pain
But let the pain be
Learn to live with it and soon I will grow beyond it
Able to handle the hurt without succumbing
Without feeding it

I left feeling light
Feeling that I could handle the separation from Ari

There was a message on my machine when I got home

A feeling of foreboding walked with me across the kitchen
Ari's voice told me she would not be able to come by
She hoped I was alright

I felt surprised as I crumbled into tears
Losing the boost from Laureen
No strength of my own to handle the let-down

An hour later Ari called
To see how I was
I stayed with my sadness
Not lashing out at her
Not blaming her for my pain

Thirty hours later she called again and
I did not do so well
After a few minutes of a shaky walk down
My lane of responsibility
I began digging at Ari
Finding reasons why she should change
Dancing carefully around outright blame
I still dumped on her
I was unable to stay with my own feelings
Twice I brought up not continuing together
My pain so hard I could not feel much difference
Between seeing her little and
Seeing her none

When I began challenging her choice
To give so much to her family
Her voice changed
I had pushed her across her line
Forcing her to protect her family
To protect her children
I felt the edge in her voice
Yet I pushed on
My pain
My numbness

My indulgence blinding me
Reason shoved aside
I argued about choices which were hers to make
Not mine

I stepped into her area of responsibility
Because I was not dealing with mine

She had to hang-up suddenly
Robert had come home
Spirit protecting us from my insanity
Limiting the damage
Or had I gone too far already
Would tomorrow bring a loss I was not sure I could survive?

I called Laureen
Desperate for another viewpoint

She told me
When two Souls who share a strong Spiritual Affinity
Come together they are like Spiritual Twins
Usually one is farther along than the other
And the one taking smaller steps
Will often choose to hold on more tightly
To their old consciousness
If one is in another relationship and
Does not leave it soon after meeting their Twin
They usually will not

She also told me Asian women raised in their culture
Will do anything to protect their children
Will do everything to keep the family together

She told me what I knew
I can push Ari and shorten our time together or
I can accept the situation and
Have as much time with her as possible
My lessons are mine to learn

"We supposedly choose our situations" Laureen said
"As we come into this life
    All the Masters I know of have had to go through
    Incredible pain
    Have had to learn to step above it
    I hope you can look into why
    You have chosen this situation to learn from"

We talked about my destructive cycles
How I hang onto my need so hard I keep Spirit out

I hung up grateful for such a good friend
Grateful to know someone who had been through more than I
Even the best words fall hollow
If unsupported by experience and knowingness

LOST POSSESSIONS

Up all night again
Reminded of my father
Awake while the world sleeps
Working to direct overwhelming creative energy
In a meaningful way
Struggling with self-created pain

The similarities thankfully stopping there
My father growing-up in an age when self-help meant
Pulling on your own bootstraps
Without regard for feelings
Or support for self-evaluation
Stuck in an ironic rut of emotional self-indulgence
Denying himself the happiness he sought so desperately
He chased away everyone he loved
Then shunned his physical body in a last vain effort
To control his world

I was his caring best friend in my last life
I was his care-taking son in this one
Free of his daily pulls for fourteen years now
Trying hard to free myself from pain captured at his side

With two hours of sleep and a knot in my heart
I slipped into Rich's office for my third appointment
Moving sideways in my vain effort to hurt less
For forty minutes I recounted the trip to Bangkok and Bali
Seeing my three lost possessions as a waking dream
"In Bangkok we began the first two mornings
   With spiritual exercises
   Then we had an early appointment on the third day
   Promising ourselves to HU when we got back to the hotel
   Instead we returned late and fell into bed
   The rest of the trip was a blur
   HUing only once or twice in the remaining ten days

"On the last night we came out of Sam's Leather Goods
Climbed into a taxi which seemed to be waiting for us
The driver a hilarious older fellow
Who wanted to take us to a "Live Show"
We declined but the thought stayed with me
He had said the girls wore no clothes
"Look but no touch" he had giggled

"Just two hours later we had to return to Sam's
For a last-minute order
The same cabbie waited outside
I suggested we go to the Live Show
Ari agreed
Intrigued if not as interested as I

"The show was horrible
Overweight young girls doing bizarre forty-second poses
Unhappy with life
Using their bodies to make a living
Depressing a dispirited crowd of hypnotized couples and
Lost single men

"We left soon thereafter
Suddenly seeing a calculating side to our cabbie
We left behind our spiritual energy as well
Having lost it in the astral mire of the Live Show

"In Bali I discovered
I had also left my copy of *Lessons Of The Heart* in Bangkok
The meaning clear

"After I returned home
I found I had left my white sandals in Bali
And failed to gather up my backgammon game
When we left the plane in Honolulu"

Rich listened quietly
Nodding with bright eyes

I continued

"I was puzzled about the sandals and backgammon
Until sitting in your waiting room

"I especially attached myself to Ari in Bali
Replaying an old pattern of refusing
To separate after once merging with a lover
My little boy hanging on desperately
All I needed to do was to stay behind a few mornings
Do my spiritual exercises and write for a couple of hours
That would have been plenty
I could not
Even though I was sick for several days
And badly needed the rest

"So losing sandals meant the loss of my independence
The loss of my higher mobility

"When we boarded to come home
We found ourselves sitting two seats away from
An employee of Ari's husband
Which meant we could not cuddle like lovers
My kid suddenly lost it
His last fifteen hours of merging with Ari taken away
I stomped and fumed
Blaming her
When she found the situation humorous
And began listening to a tape of one of Sri Thomas' talks
I unplugged her headphones
When she said 'Remember the Principles of The Path'
I said 'Fuck the Principles of The Path'"

"I know she hates the 'f' word and
I felt the sudden lowering of my vibrations

"I did not maintain my composure
I lost the game on the plane

And I know I must lose Ari
I must lose my attachment to her"

As I said these last words the pain of separation
Rolled over me and my tears drowned my voice
When I could talk again I said
"Even if she married me tomorrow
I know I would have to surrender her
Surrender our relationship to Spirit
I have to give her up
If not I will lose her
I know I have been putting my attachment for her
Before God
I can't continue this and survive as I am
What do I do now?"

Rich was quiet for a minute, then said
"It's great you have such clarity
That's usually the hard part in therapy
So let's do it
Let's HU"

I closed my eyes
Took several deep breaths and as I heard Rich's soft voice
Sing HHHHUUUUU
I too sang the Sound in all Sounds

After a few minutes Rich told me to take the HU inside
As I did he said
"Hear the HU continuing
It's a low tone
But It's where you are
Sink into It
Let It fill you with Its Sound"

I felt the vibrations of the Sound pass through me and
Slowly began to lift me
From my clogged state of consciousness

Then Rich said
"You meet the Mahanta
    Feel his love"
And I did
I felt the radiant light and love of my Inner Guide

I stayed with the feeling for a while
Then became distracted by the need for fresh air
Wondering if the vents at the bottom of the window opened
Rich closed by saying
"May the Blessings Be"
We both slowly came back to the physical

He described what I experienced
Adding how he had seen unconditional love
Pour from the Mahanta to me and then watched
As a part of my emotional body was uncovered
Standing rigid
"The frozen man
    Frozen with fear" he said
I knew what part of me he was describing

"This is your fear which you hold onto as though
    You and it have turned to ice
    Spirit is beginning now to work with you
    To soften that inner body of yours
    To bring flexibility to it once again

"You need to fall in love with the Light and Sound
    Take Spirit as your lover
    Wrap yourself in the Light
    Immerse yourself in the Sound"

I left with a small hope building
Aware that two people
Whom I knew had gone through more than I in this lifetime
Agreed with me that I must put God first in my life again and
Let Ari and all the rest of the world fall into place

As Spirit directs

As I drove home
I wondered if Ari would turn up as we planned
I wondered how she would be
I wondered what price
I would pay for my anger the night before
Knowing any price Spirit exacted would be fair

WHAT DO I THINK?

Knowing what to do
Doing it

The step from knowing to doing was clear for me yesterday
After seeing Rich
After holding Ari in my arms for forty minutes
After feeling her love

She patient with me
Having suffered after our phone conversation the night before
Feeling my pain
Feeling her own
Relieved to see
I had stepped beyond my anger

Her joy grew as I told her of my session with Rich
We parted happy lovers accepting being apart
I working hard to heal
To reach toward wholeness myself
To not depend on her for my happiness
Accepting her commitment to her family
So hard
So necessary

Later a crisis at work
Brought to a head by my sharp tongue the day before
Telling the truth
Giving back to Margie
What she gives to everyone in the office

Even if true
Impatience and no mercy do not build bonds

She had asked for a reward for solving a problem
Created by a lender
Her responsibility to avoid in the first place

I had snapped back she was saving her okole
Thanks for the good effort
But rewards are not handed out for doing your job

She left without saying good-bye to anyone
Suffering from being a sensitive person
Insensitive to how her actions affect others
And come back to her

So today she did not come in but
Called Bob to tell him she could not face the office
Not sure she could work with us

We needed her as a part of our team
She needed to grow beyond her impatience with herself
Which she turned on the rest of the world
I needed to watch my tongue
What I say so quickly manifests in my world
What I think is just as powerful
Perhaps more so because its subtlety is easily overlooked

The more I say to myself
"Ari is home with husband
  Ari is in bed with Robert
  Ari is not with me
  Ari is too busy to come see me
  She loves her family more than me
  I am lonely because she's not here
  I hurt because she's not here
  She didn't take time to call me"
The more I stir my loneliness
The more I shut down my heart and close to Spirit
Hard times follow immediately

When I chose to think
"I surrender my relationship with Ari to Spirit
  I surrender my loneliness and pain to Spirit
  I declare myself a perfect vehicle for Spirit

I understand she is doing the best she can do
I understand her love for her family
I feel her love for me
I am a happy and whole being unto myself "
I create happiness
I relieve the pressure building up inside
I open myself to Spirit
Letting it heal me

Why is guiding my thoughts so hard?

This morning I woke up after a long night's sleep
My first since returning home
Awoke into sunshine and slowly sank into oblivion
As my mind churned over the day's prospects

A slight chance of seeing Ari on her way to the shop
As she works the morning shift
Plans to see her at the store later
Perhaps having a quick lunch with her
More likely she won't be able to get away
Almost guaranteed frustration at seeing her
But not holding her in my arms

My emotional body rolled downhill from there
Unable to stop the slide of disappointing thoughts
A long HU full of rambling thoughts only softening the fall
Looking at the clock
Watching the hour slip away before she must open the shop
Calling before opening time ready to accuse and whine
No one there
Finally sitting down to write
Finding the beginning of relief as I face my process
Search for today's new thoughts
Struggling to win again the ability to choose what I think
To choose wisely

HOW CAN I DO ANYTHING BUT LOVE HER?

She did not stop by my apartment on her way to the shop
I phoned her again
Found her there and grumbled
Grumbled about her not coming by
Grumbled when I found out she left the dentist early
The day before calling me at home but not at work
When I could have told her my meeting was canceled

A lazy Friday afternoon together missed
Because she did not call me an hour after we parted
Me telling her I would be busy for several hours
I got mildly upset on the phone
More upset after hanging up
Called her back and walked the fine line
Between expressing my feelings and being a jerk

Later I bought her flowers and visited her at the shop
While she priced some of the new items
One last grumble and I shook loose from my distemper
"What can I do for you?" I asked
"Don't get mad at me and
   Make love to me"

My heart melted
My anger washed away in the runoff

Sunday morning I awoke to my alarm at 7:30
Four hours after finally getting to sleep
My body's clock somewhere east of Guam
Wanting more sleep so badly
I forced myself out of bed
Because I wanted to meet Ari at the 9:00 HU Song
Because I wanted to see her an extra hour
Because I could not call her to say I was sleeping in

As I headed to the bathroom a little voice said

"What if she calls to say she's not going?
   Are you going to be upset?"
"Probably" I admitted

A hour later
Five minutes before I was going to leave
She called
She had a headache
She would be there for the 10:00 Sunday Service

"Fine" I thought hanging up
"A headache has never kept me from seeing her"

I went to the HU Song anyway
Watching my anger break against my thoughts in small waves
"Did I really need to do this?" I asked myself
"Don't get mad at me and
   Make love to me" echoed through my inner hearing
I began softening

The HU Song opened my heart more
Afterward when I saw her car park next to mine
Half a block away in the parking lot under the big tree
I trotted down to see her
As I neared I saw no one in her car
I looked around
Then noticed her headrest was out of sight
She was laying down
Her seatback reclined

She turned her head to me as I walked up to her car
Smiling a weak smile she rolled the window down
"Hi Beauty"
"Hi Mr. Lolo"
I could see she was not in good shape
"Are you hungover?" I asked
She nodded and I climbed in on the other side of the car
I listened as she told me about the dinner

She and Robert went to the night before
About drinking champagne and wine
About having a few puffs on a cigar
About throwing-up in the lady's room
Twice

My gut tightened
I wanted to lash-out angrily
Because she had acted so stupidly
Putting distance between us
"Do you know what smoking does?" I asked
She shook her head
"It drives the Mahanta away
  For whatever reason that consciousness cannot
  Stay long in a room with cigarette smoke
  Cannot stay long with a person while they are smoking"

I wanted to hit her over her head with my words
Her actions taking her farther away from me
Then I heard her words on my inner
"Don't get mad at me and
  Make love to me"

My heart softened completely and I saw her lying there
Smiling her smile of Beauty
How could I do anything but love her?
Making her choices as she needs to
Paying her price

I recognized my insecurity
Insisting she have the same experiences as I
Needing company to validate my own choices
An old pattern
Conquered long ago
Now popping up in a moment weakened by anger

I swept my grouch aside and smiled
Had I not tested so many limits?

Didn't I still?
What's the difference between what Ari did and
When I go to a dance bar?
Both choices lower vibrations for a while
Both experiences are evidently needed by the person choosing

I reach out to her with my heart and my arms
She was not up to the Service
So I took her home for a HU for two
Then made love with her until I left her to nap
As I ran back to the Center for a local council meeting
Which I chair once a month

I could have asked someone to run the meeting for me
The afternoon before
When I learned our Sunday time together
Could run past the meeting time
Or when I saw Ari was sick
But I could not treat my new white sandals poorly
Bought with the awareness that I lost my others as a warning
A warning from Spirit that I had given up my independence
I could not put my spiritual responsibilities
Ahead of my time with Ari and
Feel like I had learned anything

When I came back from the meeting
Mercifully short and sweet
She was asleep nude on my bed
With a pillow balanced on her hips

I woke her gently asking her if the pillow was for modesty
We made love again
Then went out for Thai food
Before we left she asked me why I loved her
I thought for a moment
Searching for words that could not approach how I felt
Then said
"I love you

Because you are the other side of my heart"
She hugged me close and long
Her body's warmth so nourishing to me

Standing up slowly she looked at her watch and said
"In two minutes we will be out of here"
She hesitated
Then said "After two more minutes of kissing"
And was in my arms again
Her lips rose petals against my cheek

HOPE

Last week's trauma has melted into this week's rhythm
Manageable
Growing from work done in many little moments
Choosing carefully what I think
Watching what I do
Accepting myself when I repeat old patterns

Ari has been popping up each day
Finding ways to see me
Me finding her always subtly different
One day she's casual and I'm all over her
The next day our roles reverse

After several days of hearing from her that she was "okay"
I rebuilt my lost momentum
Left in Bali and Bangkok
Ignored amid Mr. and Mrs. Lolo's play
Smothered in my constant attachment to Ari
Suffocating from lack of spiritual exercises
I felt strong enough to ask what was beneath her surface

Tangled in the sheets of my unmade bed she smiled in my arms
I stroked her hair as she sorted her thoughts
Finally I said
"People who take longer than ten seconds
   To answer how they are
   Usually are editing their thoughts"
"Oh not me" she said
"I'm just trying to assemble my lost neutrons"
Our laughter escalated into tickling and rolling around
Then I said "Tell me really" and she did
"When you and Robert are okay I am fine
   When one of you pulls at me
   I seem to get lost in an ocean full of high waves
   Unable to sort out my thoughts or feelings
   The last few days have been smooth ones

Except for your pain
Yet I have no idea where all this is leading
Robert is growing a lot
But I'm not sure he ever will be
The spiritual person I need
At the same time I cannot imagine breaking up the family
And I worry about you
All the pain our relationship causes you "

I stroked her hair as her chin rested on my chest
Our eyes meeting for long moments then releasing
As she talked and I listened

"Robert has been very reluctant
To be close to me physically since our return
Last night he went to sleep without saying goodnight
This morning he said he got up about midnight and
Heard me talking to you on the phone
He was sad
I think he is thinking we are inseparable"

"Are we?" I asked
"What do you think, Mr. Lolo Doodoo?
Mr. Doolo"
"What a great name
And yes I think we are inseparable
Don't you agree Mrs. Doolo?"
"Inseparable in the course of eternity Mr. Doolo"

Later after sweat filled her navel
After I had given her one of her rare orgasms
She said
"I asked him yesterday how much he loved me
He said
He was not head over heels in love with me"
"How did you feel about that"
"About what I guessed"

Still later she told me Sarah had asked her that morning
"Why did you marry Daddy?"
Whatever Ari told her did not satisfy her
Sarah's response halfhearted

Ari told me the girls behave better when she is not there
They carefully avoid their Daddy's anger
She said when he gets mad at the girls he loses his love
Which they feel
"I tell Robert often
  I would rather be a little sloppy and happy
  But he seems to value discipline over love
  Over some kinds of love
  Sometimes I wonder what kind of love I have for Robert
  And what kind of love I have for you
  Do you think I'm a selfish person?
  Asking everyone to bend to my needs"

I held her closely
The length of our bodies touching
And said softly into her ear
"I think it's about time
  For you to have your needs met
  After bending to other's needs for so long
  I also think
  If we lived together
  You would find yourself hearing me say
  I would rather live sloppy and happy"

"Whatever happens you are my Zak" she said
Kissing me with fire

She had never said "my Zak" to me
Had never so fully embraced me
Loving me overwhelmingly but
Still holding back apart of herself
Not saying "my" the way lovers who live together
So dearly reach for their other half

I drove her back to her car soon
She asked me on the way
If I was building myself up to a hard fall
By talking about what it might be to live together
When she could not see that future

I told her I was focusing on growing
On trying to take each step as Spirit laid it before me
I told her my hopes got dashed periodically
Returning from this past trip was an example
Of my hopes raised without conscious thought
Being crushed
Beneath the everyday reality of not being with her

To myself I thought
My hope springs back on each of her whispers
A fool's hope perhaps

SCARED OF MY ANGER

I awoke sad this morning
Awakened early for the second morning
By a call from the Koanui family
Today it was the oldest son Kevin
Struggling with the realities of foreclosure
The family hobbled first
By Mrs. Koanui's stroke at an unexpectedly young age
Then brought to its knees when Mr. Koanui
Quit his job to care for his wife and
Let the mortgages fall seriously late

When I first met them he had yet to ask his two sons for help
Both living at home and working intermittently
I told him to be able to get a loan for him
His family would have to pull together
Not knowing it was already too late
Legal fees and prepayment penalties and higher balances
Than reported to me
Adding up to almost the value of their property

I knew a crisis loomed
Could feel it around him
I wondered if Mrs. Koanui's stroke at fifty was karma
Or the result of too many Crisco sandwiches
Mr. Koanui's eyes
Telling a story of a body overloaded with toxins
I hoped he was not next

When I hung up I stumbled into my sadness
At not hearing from Ari for forty hours
The day before I had inched my way through a long workday
And writing late into the evening
By continually refocusing on what I was doing
Thoughts of my pain took me down
Thoughts of bathing in Light and Sound leveled me
Then gently pointed me up

I worked to be a better vehicle for Spirit and
Went to bed missing her but not too down
Not at all angry with Beauty

She called
Just before I left for this week's appointment with Rich
We planned to meet in the late morning
She sounded down and unable to talk

I spent the first part of my time with Rich talking
About what I was feeling this morning
About the little steps taken throughout the past week
Then we paused and after a long moment of silence he said
"Let's talk some about your mother"
I reverberated with
"Yes! I want to talk about my mother"
I told him about how
I would rather not be talking to her these days
But was doing so a little
About my sister's apparent discomfort with
Mother's heart operation year before last and
How Jan had pulled away from Mother since then
How mother was jabbing at Jan whenever they did talk
Her anger squirting out
How my feelings echoed with Jan's especially since my visit
When I saw mother's beseeching cocker spaniel eyes
Asking me for far more than I could begin to give
About my mother telling me of her dissatisfaction
With our phone calls which I keep intentionally light and
Are now getting fewer and farther apart once again

I talked about not getting validation from my mother
That my anger had a right to exist
I no longer blamed her for leaving
But my angry kid was still pissed-off
Her usual response being
"You just have to get over that"

"You're not going to get what you what from your Mom
   Right?"
I agreed
"But you haven't given up yet
   Your little boy is still waiting"

I sat with his words for a moment then
Found myself settling into the feeling of expectation
Running silently in the background
Feverishly working to keep up with my strides

Rich talked about the incredible range of emotions possible
In a symbiotic relationship between parent and child
How the intense feelings can swing
From giving your life for the other to beyond murderous rage
And can change in a moment
I understood what he was talking about
Having experienced shifts with her which happened so fast
Without apparent reason

We talked more about validation
He brought the focus back to a comment of mine about Ari
Not validating my feelings like I want her to when I'm upset
Rich drew a distinction between caretaking for someone
Which rarely helps them grow and
Validating with love and detachment
With responsibility for each of our feelings
For each of our lives

I realized I had mixed the two kinds of validation with Ari
And I was asking my mother for something she could not give
Which would not help me grow even if she could
"This situation with your mother has been set up for a reason
   It's not a karmic hold-over
   Right?"
I knew he was right and said so

"Your little boy is holding on so tight"

"Yeah I can feel this part of me rigid with tension"
I said pointing to my solar plexus
"That's the frozen part of you we talked about last week
   That's where you lock away your fear and pain"

"I have asked in contemplation for the Mahanta to
   Take my anger take my fear take my pain
   Haven't noticed much difference so far "

"Yes of course
   It's like the story of the man who asks God
   To take his troubles for weeks and weeks
   Then finally in exasperation
   Demands to know why God hasn't helped him
   God says
'I try to take your pain from you
   But you won't let go'
   It's good you ask
   That shows your intention
   But letting go is work you have to do
   Spirit will lift the anger from you the moment
   The anger no longer serves you"

"Okay how do I let go?"
"Unconditional love
   That's what we're working on here
   You need to focus on
   Having unconditional love for your mother"
As Rich said those words I felt a circle of white light
Burst out just above my heart
I felt its heat and felt it as white light
Though I could not see it
"You have that kind of love for you Mom
   Don't you
   I just felt it in you"
I nodded
"That gives you a great starting point for this work"

We talked more about my fear of my anger
How it scared me
Having it rip out of its cage every few years when growing-up
"When I was going through my San Francisco years
  In a co-op house
  Part of the mental health system in SF
  I let my anger jump out one time without restraint
  One of my roommates whom I was a little attracted to
  But far more annoyed with
  Because of her self-center habits
  One day I yelled at her
  Just screamed in her face for about thirty seconds
  I almost got thrown out of the co-op
  That was verbal violence
  It scared me then
  It always scared me when I let out a little bit of anger
  Around my father
  He threw back ten times what I gave to him
  Felt horrible"

" I understand it's scary
  That's why we want to let it out in a manageable way
  The way a steam engine lets off excessive steam
  One of the best ways to do this is through the dream state
  Be sure and watch your dreams now
  Ask before you go to bed for help with this
  And record everything you dream
  No matter how disconnected
  Or how tired you feel waking up in the middle of the night
  To write something down"

We both were silent for a long moment, then Rich said
"Let's do a HU now okay?"

As we took deeps breathes
I felt a deep hurt surface
Felt my fright over having this anger
Felt shame at still having my anger

Unable to let it go
I cried almost silently
Slowly the HU overtook me
Soothing my tears
I held my mother's image before me as she is today and
Tried to give her love
I felt only resentment
So I rolled back the years
Saw her as I did when I was two in the early fifties
Felt a burst of love
Remembered a special feeling as a child
When seeing a particular haircut on a woman
Then later in films and TV on women in the 1950s
The same hair cut brought a mysterious warmth
I move forward in time
Decades running together on a ribbon
The rest of the fifties and the sixties were empty
Until the very end when I met her again after seventeen years
The seventies were a time of interaction
Of trying to rebuild a lost relationship
The eighties were trouble between she and I
As my life fell apart
My body unable to handle my self-abuse
My mother unable to help me
When she could not get beyond herself
Her husband and their steady relationship with martinis
Sabotaging any real growth
Big holes of no contact showed in the eighties
I went back to the early fifties and
Sank into my love for her

MAYBE I WILL

Ari arrived much later than expected
She had called once in between sounding stressed
I took her in my arms when she walked through the door
Feeling her warm heartache
I let her go and ask her how she was
As she walked toward the bathroom she said
"Depressed
  I'll be right back"

I waited for her
Hugged her again when she came out and led her to my futon

Laying down with her dress still on
Oblivious to wrinkling it
She wrapped her arms around me

"What's happened Beauty?"
She was silent
I stroked her hair waiting
Holding my breath

"The comments he's making"
  He's been making snide remarks and
  I just hate it
  Hate it!"
I felt relief pour through me
"What's he been saying?"
"Last night we worked late until midnight
  As we were going to bed he said
  'You haven't called him today have you?'
  When I said 'No' he said 'Well why don't you?'
  I said 'Maybe I will'
  It was the way he said it
  With a sneer
  How were you yesterday not hearing from me?"

I rubbed her back softly
Feeling grateful for my time with Rich
Grateful Robert was not exploding
Feeling her pain as she tries to reconcile
Her love for two men and her family
"I did pretty well during the day
  It was hard in mid-evening
  Then I pulled out of it
  Keeping my focus on being a vehicle
  I went to bed about the same time you did
  But woke up sad and disappointed with myself"

"Why are you unhappy with yourself"
"Because I didn't keep my spirits up
  I tried
  And I haven't gotten mad at you
  Just sad
  Rich said my two-year-old was pouting
  When I saw him today"

She laughed and I laughed and we both lightened up

"What happened to the Robert
  Who put you on the train for Paris?
  Who hugged you good-bye at the airport three weeks ago?"

"It seems to be okay with him for me to travel with you
  Once or twice a year
  My seeing you in town seems to be a problem"

We lay quietly for more minutes
Then I began telling her of my session with Rich
Carefully listening to her breath as I talked
Pausing for her to say something
Then going on when she did not
Finally I said
"I'm talking about myself
  Only because you aren't"

She laughed and rolled over smiling
"You're a wonderful tonic Mr. Doolo"

We did not make love
She left a while later happier
Her heart open again
Her crisis of the moment muted
Her body molding to me as we hugged goodbye

BACK TOWARD LOVE

I feel like a woodwind player blowing an unfinished reed
Of uncompromising quality
With eccentric penalties for imperfections
Sometimes forgetting to separate my lips from the mouthpiece
When I inhale
Hearing awful disharmonies
Feeling splinters sear my lips
Wondering if I'll ever develop the grace to play right
If I'll ever find the patience
To wait until the reed is finished
Before one of the splinters
Rushes into my lungs and pierces my heart

Saturday Ari was in my arms making up for Friday
Having found a two-hour opening
Between covering a shift at her shop and
Needing to join Robert and the girls at a club outing
Hating to leave me

Sunday she was free and officially with me
After Sunday Service
After a quick Thai lunch
Promising to be home by three in the afternoon
She lay in my arms in my bed until after four
Nuzzling
Talking
Holding me while I said I was feeling whiney

I could feel my little boy screwing-up his heart
Wanting more
Running the wrong words through my mind
Teasing myself into pitching a fit

But I did not
I told her what I was feeling
I felt what I was feeling without repressing it

Enjoying the relief as pressure subsided
Letting go of the hope which had crept back in
Reminding myself and sharing with Ari
Rich's comments about hope
How it was a subtle psychic manipulation
"I know to actively wish for their marriage to break up
I know that's attempting to exert psychic influence
But just hoping?" I had said to him

"Yes
It's not being neutral
Right?
Hoping is not staying with 'Whatever will be will be'
Not staying completely open to Spirit
To Its guidance"

I knew he was right but protested once more
"What about people having hope that
Carries them out of despair?"

"Depends on what they hope for and how they do it
Where they are on their spiritual path
For some people the subtle psychic influence they exert
When hoping is closer to being neutral
Than other states of consciousness they might have chosen
Can help them open more for Spirit

"For you now
Walking The Path as you are
Hope is a step backward
From where you are able to be some of the time
From that area of complete neutrality
Which is the middle road
The Path of God
What Will Be Will Be
Neither For Nor Against
Right?"

I knew he was right and agreed, adding
"I guess I am a little resistant to this one"

"Yes
   And that's OK
   As long as you are aware of it
   The sooner you are able to master this
   The smoother will be your life
   And Ari's life and her family's"

Ari and I parted that afternoon so close
Closer than I have ever been to anyone
My little boy and I kicked some rocks
Fighting back the tears as we watched her drive away
From the parking lot down the street from the Center

I went home
Took a nap
Awakened to near darkness
Sang HU and did a contemplation with all my heart
And was fine

Later I called Laureen just to say "Hello"
Feeling strong and clear
Near the end of the conversation
I blurted out
"The feeling that Ari and I will be married
   Keeps coming up"
I said it forcefully
Laureen did not say much in reply

An hour later Ari called to see if I had handled lunch
Her stomach was giving her trouble
After telling her I was okay I said
"How is it you can call me?"
Hoping to hear she was able to talk
Instead she said she was just putting Sally to bed
Telling me with those words she couldn't talk

Then I heard Sally ask "Who is it Mommy?"
Suddenly she was on the phone saying "Hi Zak"
In a voice so loving and sweet my heart crumbled

Ari came back on the phone and hung up with a quick good-bye

My declaration to Laureen about marrying Ari
Ari's brief phone call and
Sally's sleepy voice
Made quick work of my supposed stability
Sending me to bed at the end of my evening
Blinded to what I had let loose in myself

I awoke in the morning on edge
Hearing Ari tell me over and over
Robert had not touched her for two days after coming home
So she finally made love to him
After which he hugged her like before she left

She not perfectly wise to tell me that detail
I less wise to stir my hope
Turning from Spirit's firm voice
Feeding the flames of my discontent

I worked hard through my morning disciplines of
Physical and spiritual exercises
To calm my emotional unrest
Leaving in time to catch her as she arrived at the shop

Wanting to see her
Needing to see her
Using an article in Newsweek on "Words Which Wound"
As my reason for being there
My self-deception hiding the simple truth
I did not need an excuse to surprise Ari
She was always happy to see me

In her car in the parking lot
I told her I was fine
Trying to handle my discomforts myself
Trying to hide their causes too
Foolishly

In less than five minutes I was out of the car door, saying
"Which means I'm not worth a full-time relationship
  Right?"
Ignoring her pleading "That's not what I said"
Running to my car
A white-hot poker up my okole
Self-inflicted

The path out of the garage leading by her car as
She was straightening her car in the stall
I stopped blocking her in
Jumped out of my car and back into hers
Yelling that she had no idea how much I hurt

Ari snapped back that I had no idea how she hurt
We were off like racehorses
Giving unseen irony
To the magazine article still laying in my car
Each trying to outrun our pain
Each trying to blame the other

She reached a new level in acting out
Perhaps hitting my norm
Surprising me with her bitterness and self-destruction
"I'm a selfish bitch
  Why don't you just forget me and find someone else
  I'm just manipulating you and Robert to get what I want"
She became determined and more creative after that
I stopped
I cried
"Why are you crying?" she demanded
"Because I hurt" I said through my tears but stopped crying

I began my rescue of her but it had little effect
"I'm no Beauty" she said when I called her that

We sat in her car for an hour
While her shop stayed unopened
Me pleading laughing soothing
Trying anything I could think of to turn her back toward love

Finally I had to leave for an appointment
She had to open the store
We parted with a hug and long faces
But much better than minutes earlier

I was late for my meeting at the office
My client calling in
Finding me not there and then not at his house
When I called him back

I spent most of an hour writing a letter to Ari
Knowing I had to make a strong effort to help her heal
Feeling dull dumb and lifeless
Knowing I had caused our fight
She had been bright and delighted to see me
When I first arrived

I left work in a mad dash
Found a new flower shop that took American Express
My cash flow drying up again
My old flower shop now only accepting Visa and MasterCard
My Visa almost full
Bought twenty-four red roses and a dozen lavender ones
Raced down to Ari's shop
And waited outside for a customer to leave
And waited
A friend walked by said "Those look like an apology"
Pointing to my armful of roses
We laughed
I said Spirit was making me wait as I watched Ari's customer

Try on her zillionth pair of earrings
She and Ari laughing too

Then the woman left and walked three steps out the door
Turned around and walked right back in
Seeing her leave I began to move toward the shop
Seeing her turn around I canceled the instructions to my legs
I just jerked spastically

The woman left again just as two other women went in
I watched accepting my own creation

Then the store was empty
I walked in
Ari smiled her smile of Beauty
She was fine
I was amazed
Gave her my letter
We talked in calm rational tones
About what had happened
About our love
An hour later after several shuttles in and out of the shop
To give customers space
Ari walked me to her car so we could touch to say good-bye
"Here we are again" she said
Underling my determination to stay cause and not react again

We talked more frankly than in the store
Both expressing our feelings
I found out I had hurt her deeply when I said that
Growth was a low priority in her family
I had thrown it at her in the heat of my pain
Now I wasn't sure if I meant it or not
So I supported her hurt without getting into more conflict

I still don't know what I think
Except it is not my business and
It surely is not a neutral thought

We parted lovers again though both aching some
Both forgetting about my letter

By nightfall I could no longer stay at work
My body struggling with a cold
Everything at the office falling apart
I went home and wailed for an hour
Deep guttural cries coming in waves like projectile vomit

I wondered if I was crying for Ari
Or my mother
Or had I begun to let go of my anger
And was now entering the grieving process
Rich had said I would experience when I finally realized
I would not be getting what I wanted from my mother
Or Ari
Or anyone else in the outer

What I wanted was to be back home with God
I knew this even through my tears
But they kept coming
Finally I called Laureen
She wasn't in but called back soon

Good friends
Wise friends know when to listen
When to suggest
When to be point-blank
Laureen listened then did not waste words
"There comes a time in a person's unfolding
  When Spirit will no longer let them lean on anyone
  You are at the point
  It's a hard lesson and it's a wonderful lesson
  You can't lean on anyone except the Mahanta
  My dear friend
  I would hurt for you if it would help
  Because I am foolish when it comes to helping those I love

Even though I have gone through what you are going through
But I won't
I'll just love you
You're a beautiful Soul and you will be more beautiful and
A better vehicle when you master this lesson"

I went to bed early
Tired
Grateful for Laureen's help
Knowing the work she has done in her life
Feeling Spirit come through her to help me

I fell asleep quickly and woke suddenly a couple hours later
Thirsty
As I was putting down the glass of water in the kitchen
I heard a key in the door
Nude and startled I stepped behind the door and opened it
Peering around the edge
Ari stared back at me key in hand and slid into the apartment

We grabbed each other and held on
Then ran for the bed slipping under the covers

She was more open to me than she had ever been
Telling me she was worried she had pushed me away earlier
With her harsh words of pain
We made love all in the same motion as we undressed her
She stayed with me wrapped into one until she had to go
I said I would walk her to her car
She invited me to come to her shop

Robert's three glasses of wine
The need for one of them to drive a friend home from dinner
Her need to pick up some sold items at the shop
So she could mend them in the morning
All combined to make our time together possible

I rode with her through the almost empty streets of Honolulu

As torrential rain wrapped us in a magical cocoon
Relishing the nighttime with her
We enjoyed each other's company
As she fixed the blouse at the store
Then kissed for long minutes in her car
In the parking lot under my apartment

Watching her drive away
I repeated to myself "I cannot lean on anyone"
Hearing Spirit's full orchestra playing on the inner

PATH TO FREEDOM

"I cannot lean on anyone"
Rolled through my mind for the next day and a half
"Is life really this alone?" I wondered

I took the question into contemplation

Slipping out of my body in a way so subtle and familiar
I did not realize I was doing so
For the first several years of contemplating
I found the Mahanta on the inner
Waiting for me in his shimmering light-soaked body
Resembling the physical body of Sri Thomas
The Spiritual Leader of The Path
Who today carries the Mahanta Consciousness

In the higher worlds of pure Spirit beyond the mind
Soul does not bother with lower world forms
To present to me the image I can most easily accept
The Mahanta usually appears in a near-physical body

We sat in a warm room full of blue light
Looking up I saw only stars where a ceiling might have been

"Feeling alone?" he asked me in his direct gently way
"Well not at the moment!" I laughed
"What does that tell you?"
I thought for a minute
Still in the lower planes
Still using my mind for communication
But now in a rarified environment
My thoughts were able to form
Unhampered by the demands of my physical body

I saw the answer dancing before me
I was feeling alone because
I was closed down to my inner guide

To the Mahanta and all his vast resources
"Guess I'm shut down some
  What do you suggest?"
"Asking is helpful
  Asking again and again
  Remembering I am always with you
  All you have to do is open to the Light and Sound"

"Right" I said out loud in my physical body
Opening my eyes to a burst of white sparkles
Surrounded with the echo of his words
"I am always with you"

"I will only lean on the Mahanta" I said
Knowing this was my path to freedom

WORDS THAT WOUND

A few hours later Ari was in my arms for our Wednesday lunch
She was feverish in her passion

Telling me later she had shown my letter to Robert
I stiffened expecting a new problem

"What's wrong?
   Did you not want me to do that?"
"It's your letter to do with what you want
   What did he say?"
"He said it made him feel better
   Feel more positive about you
   He said he was glad I got angry with you too
   He said maybe he should invite you out for a drink"

"Great
   I hope that doesn't happen"
"He was joking
   He knows you don't drink"
"Good"
"He also said he wanted to come to the Sunday Services"

My heart froze
How could I say no?
How could I handle him being there?
Then I realized the real issue was
How could I deal with
Watching them drive away together each Sunday
Losing our so-recently-won Sunday afternoons together

I could feel tears threatening

"But he said he could not face you" Ari spoke quietly
"How do you feel about that?" I asked my voice husky
"About like you do
   From what I see in your eyes

I feel awful that any part of me
Would even think about standing in his way
I could not tell him not to come
I must do all I can to help him grow
Right?
But it would be so hard on me to be there with you both
And to lose our Sundays together"

She was quiet for a moment then said
"He said he could not face the people there"
We looked into each other's eyes
Feeling our sadness
Feeling Robert's sadness

Ari spoke with a quiver in her voice
"The more time I spend with you the more I miss you and
The less I feel toward Robert
I feel dull toward him now
When he holds me I don't feel anything
I'm scared"

I held her
"What are you scared of"
"Change I guess
Change and hurting people"

My mind thought of many things to say to her
But I let them all go
Sensing she needed love not thoughts
We held each other as the early afternoon sun
Passed beyond my window
Her tears flowing across her cheek and dripping on mine
Feeling like a cherished offering

A little later she said "I wrote you a note"
Pulling from her pocket a small square of paper
I unfolded it
"You had better read this" I said

Looking at small writing in faint pencil

She took the note and read
"Dearest Zak
    Past midnight, 2:12 am
    My heart aches with longing for you
    How I could love you
    Tears stream down my cheeks
    My desire for life and spiritual growth feels uncontrollable
    Yet I can't let go of my reasoning mind
    Not wanting to be a selfish creature
    Choosing you means spiritual growth
    Recognition of my self-purpose

    "Staying on means being faithful
    How could I leave him
    After so many years of depending on him
    I chant HU like crazy
    I chant ZZZZand
    I chant I surrender
    I surrender
    Tears still run down my cheeks"

She left later saying
"I feel better
    I always feel better when I see you"

We kissed in the parking lot
She rushed off to her many things to do
I rushed back to work

In the evening after my new telephone surveyor
Had finished her third evening
Still using words without a clear idea of their meaning
I went home and turned on my computer
Pulling up the letter I had written to Ari on Monday
The letter she had shown to Robert
Giving him a more positive feeling about me

What had I said to cause his change?
Was he still knowing me only from the two phone conversations
He taped in April when I was so low
Pulling at Ari in my worst way?

I read the letter

"Dearest Beauty

"How ironic that on the day I bring you a magazine article
  Entitled *Wounding With Words*
  I wound you with my words

"When I let my anger take control
  I lose my spiritual awareness
  Close my heart and become an idiot
  I see my actions affecting you more each time too

"When you get down I am able to absorb your pain usually
  Without it bringing me down
  Because you don't often strike out to wound me
  When you hurt
  Or strike out blindly having the same effect
  Maybe you want to do this as much as I
  Only you have better self-control

"I sometimes have the behavior of a child
  It's a part of me I am working to grow past
  Obviously I have not healed this part of me yet

"Today when I got angry I saw you turn your anger
  Inward then outward then inward again
  This is your dynamic to sort out
  As your complicated life allows
  I can offer you my support when I am able and promise
  To keep trying my best not to hurt you

"You can do no more than you can do

The same is true for me
Much of the time we are able to meet in the middle ground
Sometimes not
If you want to no longer see me I cannot change that
I also cannot change the love I have for you

"The farther anyone goes on The Path
The quicker their actions come back to them
Sometimes that pace is bewildering
I was bewildered today
Seeing my anger induced pain come back immediately

"I would rather see you and I apart
With you happy
Than for us to be together as lovers-when-we-can
And for you to self-destruct like I watched you do today

"You have a tremendous amount of worth
As a person and as Soul
My words won't have much meaning to you until you agree
This is one of the lessons of The Path
Each of us learning our own self-esteem
Sri Thomas has said several times that the only 'sin'
If there is one at all
Is holding onto low self-worth
I know this well and is why I am working
To clear out my garbage and
My feelings of very low self-worth

"Take a deep breath and
Try to open your heart again Beauty
My love is always with you
Sometimes it does get buried under my unrecycled garbage

"My deepest apology to you
The Beauty of my life
For losing it so badly today

Love Zak"

I turned off my computer
Sat quietly listening to the traffic outside
Feeling my love for Ari
Feeling hope
Which I knew was only a sign of more inner work
Yet to be done

A DREAM OF GIBBERISH

"Last Friday after I left here
    I kept my attention on the Mahanta
    Better than I normally do for a Friday Fast"
I said to Rich
"The mental fast?" he asked
"Yes
    I find I am able to stay in balance better
    When keeping my thoughts on the inner
    On my inner guide the Mahanta
    Than having just one meal or drinking only juice
    Some days I only have one meal but
    That's when my body asks to eat just once"

"Why don't you keep your attention
    On the Mahanta every day?"

Rich's question was not easy to answer
I was beginning my fifth session with him
Sitting in his office feeling a partial sense of home
Our trust and friendship broadening step by step
Into a working relationship

"I do when I can
    I like making a special effort one day a week"
I was quiet
Wondering with images instead of words
Whether to admit to myself how little I was "successful"

"I probably should add that 'making a special effort'
    To keep my focus on the Mahanta
    Means increasing it from ten seconds
    Every once in a while throughout the day
    To ten seconds two or three times that often"

"What do you think the Friday fast means?" Rich asked me

"Thinking about the Mahanta all the time"

"Could you do any work?
Could you carry on a conversation
Thinking about something else constantly?
Even the Mahanta"

"I don't seem to have mastered that yet"

"I don't know of anyone who has
Keeping attention on the inner
On the Mahanta or whoever is your inner guide
To me means nurturing an attitude of openness and love
Toward your personal way-shower
The same way you carry your love for Ari"

"I guess I know this on some level"

"I am sure you do
It's easy for our minds to get so involved in our lives
Simple efforts are made into complex ones"

Rich paused, then said
"Let's talk about your dreams for a minute
Were you able to remember any?"

"Yes
When I went to bed last Friday night
I did a contemplation asking to remember my dreams
Promising to awaken and record them
Promising to write them down the next day
Then when I got into bed I asked to be taken
To where I could best learn what I needed for my next step

"All things I have known to do for quite a while
Just haven't done very often"

"And..."

"And I remembered three dreams each of which I described
  Into the little tape recorder I keep by my bed
  And I wrote them up later"
I pulled out two pages of copy
Ground out by my dot matrix printer that morning

"Would you like to read them?" Rich asked

The first was four lines of gibberish
The second was concerned with
Not getting sexually involved with a woman
Because I did not want to break the bond with Ari
In the third I became aware my baggage
Was following me at a distance

After I read the dreams Rich finished taking notes then said
"Let's go back over them line by line
  Read the first one again"

I read
"Trying to write to freeze instinct
  Looking up the skirt of a young virgin girl
  I hope she does not kill me
  I'm trying to write this in Thai"

"What does the first line mean to you?" Rich asked

"When I awoke I knew I had three dreams
  I remembered recording them at three different times
  But I did not remember these words
  Spoken in the middle of the night"

"Which shows the value of
  Making the kind of commitment you made that evening
  Right?"
"Sure does"

"Read the first line again"
I did and Rich said
"Was that 'freeing'?"
"No
freezing, freeze"
"What could that mean?"
"Well to me it means holding something in place
Which wants to escape"
"Who's the best authority on your dreams?"
"I am"
"Right
When someone else gives you feedback on a dream you share
What do you do?"

"Oh I ignore it completely" I said laughing
Rich laughed too, then said
"Many times that's a great idea
What happens for you to be able to
Accept what someone else says?"
"I get a knowingness inside
It clicks in
Something on the inner says 'Yes this is truth'"

"Me too
That's how I operate
The second line of your dream
Read that again"

I read "Looking up the skirt of a young virgin girl"

"What does that mean to you?"
"It was really hard to share with Ari
I thought she would think I was a terrible person
Unfit to be with her girls"

"Did she?"

"No

She was very loving"

"Do you feel an attraction for her daughters?"

"Yes
A strong one but nothing sexual
They are two special kids I loved from the beginning
Like I had known them all their lives"

"Where do you think this part of the dream comes from?"

"Well I have been choosing not to fantasize much lately
Doing so seems to keep awake the part of me
Which seeks titillation"
I paused looking deeper inside then continued
"When I have fantasized about sexual situations
I've found the women are getting younger"

"How young?" Rich asked
"Mid to late teens"
"Anyone specific?"
"No
Just imagined female bodies"
"Do you tie-in 'looking up the dress' with
'freezing instincts'?"

I thought a minute
I had not connected the two
"Not until now
But it makes sense"

"Freud was really caught up in freezing his instincts
With his Oedipus tendencies"

"I don't want to play out this forty-year-old need
For the body of a young woman"

"With your awareness and

By keeping these feelings flowing through
You don't need to
Freud couldn't let go of his obsession
So he had to spend most of his life focused on this issue
You don't have to do that
You also have your inner guidance to lean on "

"Yes and I'm lucky I've had enough experiences to know
The needs of the body are so momentary"

"So let's build on this
The third line about killing you
Read that"

I was shaken
Opening up about these impulses for the first time
Opening to Rich another degree
I read the third line "I hope she does not kill me"

"Who is she"

"The girl?
Ari?
My mother?"

"All parts of your feminine side
As you are beginning to let go of your frozen self
You will regress gradually
Your attraction to younger women
Is your natural opening to the feminine energy you lost
When you split from the feminine part of yourself"

"Which is part of my draw to Ari's girls?"
"Of course"
"And to my nieces
Whom I spent a lot of wonderful time with
When they were growing up?"
"Right"

"Is this like rebirthing?"

"There are many ways to heal ourselves
Some involve regression
Going back to repair old wounds
Some regression is done consciously
Some in the dream state
Some in other levels of the inner worlds
Rebirthing is usually too sudden
It takes someone from where they are today
Back to childhood to the source of this lifetime's hurts
Then returns them to today's reality too quickly
Without the in-between support
Without allowing Spirit
To handle this part of our lives by It's timetable

"Your will or my will or any person or entity's will
Only adds to the confusion
It takes the guidance of Spirit--or God by any name
To lead us through the lower inner worlds
Some levels of which are full of entities
Who have a wide spectrum of agendas"

Rich and I both took a breath
I felt the sunshine coming through his office window

"This one's a doosey isn't it?" Rich laughed
"Sure is"
"Read the last line"
"I'm trying to write this in Thai" I said

"What does that mean to you?"
"That I'm struggling to communicate
In a language I have not Mastered
And to write in Ari's language"

"Okay
How about we go on to the next dream" Rich suggested

My mind was anxious to get busy again but
My heart felt banged up from the feelings passing through
"No let's don't" Rich said
  There's a lot here
  Right?
  Let's relax and go inside first "

We closed our eyes and sang HHHHUUUUU softly
I could feel energy swirling underneath my solar plexus
Pushing up and around it some but mostly churning below
Stuck and trapped

Rich's HU fell silent
Soon he spoke
"The old hurts you hold in your stomach area
  Prevent energy from flowing up through your chakras

"Let the pure white light of Spirit flow through you now
  Soaking into the knot of energy you hold
  Massaging this blockage
  Releasing some of the energy to go free
  Hear the sound of the HU ringing through you
  Breaking up the blockage"

As with many spiritual exercises
Where I place my attention determines my experience
I can turn my focus
Toward the Light and Sound of Spirit anytime
But so often do not
Caught up in my every day tensions

Hearing Rich's words
I felt a golden-white light pour through me and
Drank it in with each breath
Soaked it up through my skin
Embraced it with my opening heart

Then I felt the sound of HU surge

Becoming a piercing howl
Hammering away at the watermelon-sized chunk of debris
Always with me
Always in my gut

The urgent HU stopped
Replaced again with a soft loving HU
Accompanied by the echo of several violins

Rich said "May the Blessings Be"
My eyes opened
My mind jumped ahead spewing words
"That's why!
   That's why my sexual energy is so hard to handle!"
Rich smiled and nodded his head knowing exactly what I meant

Realization poured through me
My long-ago trauma as a child
A situation I chose as Soul before this lifetime
To provide motivation to learn
From which I shrank wanting to avoid more pain
Holding my fear
Creating an intimate relationship instead
With the very pain I so wanted to avoid
Causing a blockage in my guts
Keeping my sexual energy trapped
Not permitted to flow up
Not allowed to transform into purer energy
Not able to nurture my higher chakras
Causing my fixation with sexuality soon after puberty
Causing the incredible awakening into anguish
When I fell in love at seventeen
Only to see it fall apart six months later
Firing my search for love in all the wrong places
Beginning my infatuation with titillation
In the dark seats of Cinema Arts on Franklin Street
Watching old west cowboys cross a corral full of tire tracks
To watch the rancher's daughter undress in the barn

Knowing she had an audience
Wanting what was inside
The zippered jeans of the handsome cowhand
Standing at the barn door

Watching these films
Energy blasting from my crotch
I took the pleasure and ran from my old pain
Ran into all the dark places I could stand
Creating an addiction to titillation
Because my sexual energy had nowhere else to go
Because I could not sit with it
Because I wanted to escape

Why would I choose this path?
What did Spirit and I agree this would teach me?

Rich told me he could see my lower chakra energy
Beginning to come up and around my blockage
Flaring in swirls
"As you consciously work with the Sound and Light
  You will find your energy patterns changing
  This kind of change can happen in a moment
  But only if you are ready and Spirit directs
  Time is not the issue
  Awareness is
  You can take as many lifetimes as you choose
  To work through this"

I left walking on a razor's edge
Wanting to take this step now
Not wanting to wait a moment longer but knowing
Surrender to Spirit's timetable is vital
To develop greater balance and avoid further karmic tangles

Getting into my car
I felt the sunshine and heard a distinct HU

Coming from some hidden building machinery close by

SEX OR ALCOHOL

It was like being given a key
Unlocking the unknown
The awareness of what I had learned in Rich's office grew
Providing new insight into many experiences
Giving me an important piece
In the puzzle of my sexual rampage

Soon after I came to Hawaii and referred by the
Jin Shin Jyutsu practitioner I had been seeing on the mainland
I began getting treatments from Laureen

I had enjoyed my previous practitioner
For her spiritual awareness
As much the balancing I felt from the treatments
It had been hard to leave her

Resistant when I first met Laureen
Still attached to my friend who suggested I see her
I waited for three months before making an appointment

After my initial reserve was washed away by Laureen's love
By the amount of Spirit pouring through her
I found a new friendship growing
With roots deeper than I imagined
Within a few months I was discussing my sexual flows
How the energy buffeted me around

Laureen had cautioned me
"Hawaii has an overabundance of sexual energy
   We are one of the closest points to the Astral
   In the physical world
   The Islands have a long history of free sexual attitudes
   And the old energies from Lemuria still linger in this area
   Be careful and be aware

"The sexual energy can be brought up

Into the higher chakras and transformed into Spirit
If people are not able to do so and lose it here
They lose it to either sex or alcohol"

I tried bring the energy up from my base chakra
With no success
When the subject came up again with Laureen
She was surprised I had not mastered it
Ashamed and barely able to talk about my experiences
I shut-up and continued trying to solve the riddle
Without stopping to hear the question

A year later she gave me a book about
The Taoist Art of Cultivating Male Sexual Energy
The author talked about his experiences with
Having sex but not orgasms
Pointing out that just shutting down the natural release
Was painful and harmful
Guiding that energy to release inside the body
Was rejuvenating and built strength

I tried some of his exercises and was able to feel
My sexual energy rise from my base chakra up my spine
Over my crown chakra
Down passed my throat and heart and into my navel
Completing the cycle
I worked with this discipline for a few weeks and
Felt the beginning of a renewal of my deep energies

Then I lost the rhythm in one of my raids on the dance bars
Shattering all my disciplines and setting back my health

To now connect the blockage in my gut
With the anger I hold toward my mother and probably father
To see how this dynamic was holding me back from
Better handling my situation with Ari
Preventing me from giving her the smooth flow of love
I so wish to give

Seeing that the path to releasing the stuck energy
Is through giving unconditional love to my mother
Doing so the best I can
Feeling the blockage begin to dissolve
Feeling the resulting added grief
Of what I have so long avoided feeling
I have a new commitment to staying with the bubbling
Tickling energy I so often feel below my navel
The churning in my loins often lashed into a fever
By the stark titillation available in Honolulu

Able now to raise some of the energy to a higher state
So clearly seeing the choice
Between perpetuating an old habit and taking my next step
I have been able to work with this part of myself
With new understanding and success

I feel like cheering
I feel so grateful
I feel so much closer to the Mahanta
Opening more
As I let go of a slice of the concrete watermelon in my gut
Leaning on my inner guide when I need to
Able to blunt my anger at Ari for not meeting my needs
By saying to myself
"Mahanta I will lean on only you"

A SURPRISE

Much of the weekend was spent
With the Koanuis and the Malanos
Acting as facilitators while the Koanuis came to grip
With selling their home to prevent foreclosure auction
Having a difficult time
With Mr. Malano's small-eyed tightness
As he gave the family in foreclosure no break
In purchase or lease-back terms

My Sunday time with Ari was a wonderful break in the weekend
My new ability to handle my feelings and
Be a vehicle no matter who was involved
Smoothed my full days and empty nights

Soon after I got to the office on Monday
I was told someone had arrived to see me
Waiting in the conference room downstairs

Walking into the room hoping to see Ari
I was amazed at the blond women standing next to her bicycle
Beside the conference table
"Hello Gwen" I said wondering what could have brought
My errant local editor back into my world

She acknowledged her audacity and asked about the book

"It's in deep limbo
   Half revised and mostly forgotten
   I'm working on other stuff"
Remembering as I spoke
She had a financial interest in the book
If it was published with her editing intact
If she had completed her contract after she was paid in full

I pushed down strong impulses to tell her to get the hell out
And waited

She looked more masculine and angular than the year before

"I have to be able to do this"
She said to herself in a stage whisper then paused
"If it's money I don't have any extra" I said
"That's it
  I need a certain sum by 4:30 today to keep my home
  My motorcycle is in the shop
  I can put that up as collateral"

I wanted to tell her she had burnt her bridge a year ago
To point to the ludicracy of asking me for money now
When she would not speak to me
The few times I had seen her in the health food store
Since she abandoned her editing
Instead I said "It's not an option Gwen"

"You are doing OK?" she asked
"I have a lot of work to do and cash flow is low right now"
"And you have a roof over your head and a car?"
"Yes" I said and said no more

After a long moment she wheeled her bike around and
Moved out of the conference room
As she left I said "I wish you well" and meant it
I also knew
I would not support her unique brand of need again

CURIOUSLY MISSING URGENCY

As the blockage in my gut dissolves faint whisper by whisper
New energy comes through and
I have felt again what I think is the absence of need
Or the lessening

My desperation for Ari is muted
Leaving love unvarnished
I remember feeling this for a brief time during the summer
Remember how it felt similar to past times
When my need for a woman ended and
I ran from the relationship
Left with only the hollow shell of love unformed

Now the love is strong
If also stressed by the situation
Now when most of the need vaporizes
I am left with a feeling of curiously missing urgency
So long associated with love

LONGING FOR SIMPLICITY

Robert left town for two days
Opening the way for a fun evening with Ari Sarah and Sally
We ate at my and the girls' favorite Mexican restaurant
Then spent a twenty-dollar hour at the Fun Factory

Quite a treat for a school night
Sarah was open and loving to me
Indulging in only one small dig at dinner
Sally was rascally and roly-poly in her affection
But had a hard time living up to the bargain made earlier
She had agreed to let Ari and me go to a late movie
In return for the mid-week treat of the Fun Factory
"But you and Daddy left us here Monday night
   After we got dressed up and he said we weren't invited"
She complained to Ari as we drove the girls home
I wished so much I was her Daddy

Ari soothed Sally for a long time
We waited for them to fall asleep
Debating about which if any movie to see
Raced finally to the mall
Cuddled in the back row of a nearly deserted theater
Then left an hour later to go to my apartment
To cuddle without restriction

The next morning Ari called and talked about being torn
Between feeling responsible for her girls and
Leaving them alone to be with me
We talked about how it was different
When she and Robert left Sarah and Sally alone
Because they shared the decision
When she left them to be with me
She felt she was shirking her responsibility
And torched with fear of anything happening

She talked about how her values were changing

About how complicated her life is
I said
"People's lives often get complicated because
   They try to fill their needs outside themselves"
She agreed and said the house they were building
Important to them two years ago
To attract friends
To have as an accomplishment and a status symbol
No longer held the same value to her

She told me about being up late one night
Having seen part of a movie about a woman who was an artist
Who had a lover a husband a son and
Lived by herself on a cliff in Scotland

Ari said she did not want to go to that extreme but
She longed for the free time to do the work she feels in her
She longed for a simpler life in a simpler place
She said it does not take much money
To meet her needs these days
But she's stuck in a cycle of high expenses

She talked about going to a party
And how the social functions are less and less fun for her
The last one had been somewhat interesting because
The people at her table shared their spiritual outlooks

I said to her that no matter where you go
If you go thinking about giving
Of being a vehicle for Spirit
Then it doesn't matter if you enjoy your time or not
I said
"I often had a hard time keeping this attitude
   But I'm aware of it and
   I know its possible to experience"
"Yes
   That sounds right to me"

LOVE AND RISK

The next morning as I was exercising
She stopped by early and unexpectedly
Having spent the evening before with her girls
Just Mommy and Sarah and Sally

After a warm hello kiss she stretched across my futon asking
"Can a man have so much love in him and not show it?"

I had been up three hours writing and contemplating
Before doing acu-yoga and hopping onto my rowing machine
My mind was having a full-stride morning
"There are all kinds of love and all kinds of men"
I said words pouring out of me like sweat
"Some like my father are full of love and need
   But are not able to give in a true sense
   To take the risk to open themselves

"Sex and need draw us into a relationship
   In which we can grow or hide
   If we take the risk to grow and to open
   We learn about love
   Loving to give
   Loving without expectation
   Neutral love
   Then opening more and more to divine love"

"I think I started in the middle and have gone backward"
"How so?"
"Last night I wrote in my journal and
   Read a section I had read while on the ship last summer
   Missing your touch
   Needing you
   When I compare how I feel now
   To how I felt about you last year before we became intimate
   I think I have gone backward"

I took both of her hands and held them in mine
Looking at her gently curving fingers
"Last year you were a spectator watching from the bleachers
   This year you are vulnerable yourself
   My father would have argued violently
   Against the thought he was on the sidelines
   'How can I be on the sidelines and hurt this much?'
   He might have said
   If we had ever been able to have a conversation like this
   But hurting so much is what keeps people on the sidelines
   Holding that hurt in
   Holding the pain in so hard they cannot fathom risk"

"Do you think I have been on the sidelines?"
"I know my father was
   He wanted to play his game his way
   Which must have been what he needed in this lifetime
   I'm sure you have had the experiences you most needed
   And yes I think you have been living on the sidelines
   Especially when comparing your life now with before
   You are risking this year"

"I risked last year!"
"What did you risk last year?"
"I risked my heart with you
   My wonderful lover turkey"

Our talk ended and our communication increased

STAYING CAUSE

Our cash box downstairs used for soda and snack money
Was emptied of its fifty dollars last week
Presumably by one of the appraisers-in-training
Working for our new downstairs tenants
Several of whose income is moment-to-moment

Bob asked me to put a lock on the pantry door one evening
After doing so I phoned him to find out
Where he would like me to hide his key
Or should I keep it until I saw him next

The first I heard from anyone in the office
Was a call from Margie the next morning
Asking me "Where'd you hide the key?"
I told her I still had it
Bob had not called back to me to tell me where to hide it

"What do you need out of the pantry?" I asked
"Some people like to gets snacks from there in the morning"
I told her I would be there in a couple of hours
"Can you wait that long"
"I suppose so"

A few minutes later I realized Margie was probably saying
"I want a snack from the pantry"
I jumped in my car and drove the few blocks to the office
Hair uncombed
Wearing old purple plaid cotton pants
And an older stained purple t-shirt
With last week's wrinkled green business shirt
Thrown over my shoulders

I walked in to humorous comments
By people upstairs and down
Went straight to Margie at her desk and said
"Here's the key to the pantry

See you again in a couple of hours"
"Okay"
No thank you or any pleasant greeting

I started to react but said nothing
Determined to let Margie be Margie
Driving home I shed my reaction
Knowing I had not taken the key to the office for praise but
To help her and anyone else who wanted a snack

An hour later she called me at home to relay a message
From the Commissioner
On the Malano's purchase of the Koanui foreclosure
She did not have to take the time
I would have been at the office in another hour
After I called the Commissioner from home
After I had plunged back into writing
Finished and was in the shower
I saw how my staying Cause with Margie
Not reacting to my unmet need of being thanked
Had opened the way for a positive exchange between her and me

I saw how staying Cause
When I can do so
Makes my life more workable and less painful
Helping me to be open and a better vehicle for Spirit

MAMILANI

Ari called in the afternoon
Twenty minutes before I had to leave for an appointment
At just the time I had told her twice the day before
Would be a good time to end a visit not start one
If she could arrange her day to do her errands in the morning

On the phone she said she was coming into town for errands
After I told her I was just leaving for an appointment and
Might be back about five
Said she would have to be home about the time I got back
With no reference to my request of the day before

I asked her to hold and called Mrs. Kim
To see if we could postpone our appointment for two days
She was still at work and agreed
I switched back to Ari and said "I can make it"
"You postponed..."
"Yes but it was just a preliminary interview
Rescheduled for Wednesday when you will be on Maui"
I stuffed down my disappointment
She had not remembered my schedule
Had not even acknowledged
She was unable to shift her day around to match mine
Focusing only on wanting to see her

We spent half the afternoon in mad flight around town
In pursuit of things for her shop and the new Picture Store
Scheduled to open that week in the Ritz Carlton on Maui
Office supplies
Cash register
Printing
Light fixtures
Display shelving
Buying some looking some

At the last stop to pick-out shelving

Ari sounded rude and demanding
When she asked the large sad woman behind the counter
"Is there an expert here!"
Without finding out if the woman knew the stock well
"There is but she quit last week" the woman replied

Ari had the brittle tone in her voice I had heard before
My skins crawled when I heard it
She sounded impatient and condescending
Mired in her mind
Forgetting to open her heart
Forgetting to see the person across the counter as Soul
I pushed down my feelings
Read the card business cards stacked on the register and
Asked the woman if her name was Mamilani
"We don't set out cards of people who don't work here"
She said in her sad way
The deep folds and lines in her face
Reminding me of a huge gentle basset hound
I joked with her
When we left I made sure to say a warm
"Good-bye Mamilani
  Thanks for your help"

Knowing Ari was late to pick up Sarah for her piano lesson
I drove us straight back to my office
No time left over for a quick stop by my apartment
To hold each other as lovers

Sitting in the car she did not seem in a hurry to leave

I felt myself sliding down
Disappointed we could not be together fully
Not knowing when I would see her again
Maybe not until the weekend with her trip to Maui coming up
Unable to say
"I feel so low
  Missing you all the time

You are so busy
You can't even remember my schedule
Seeing you so harried and mental
Heart closed to other people
I would like to cry
I hurt so much being away from you "

I could not say that
Somewhere my mind said
"Those feelings aren't allowed
You know the situation"
So I dumped junk on her
Told her how hard it was not to see her
How hard it was to go to sleep every night
Knowing who she was choosing over me
Telling her the consciousness
She worked so hard to keep intact with Robert sucked
"But you want it don't you" I said
Trying to rub her face in her choices which hurt me so much

I said these words quietly
Sadly
Not yelling in anger
But still jabbing at her

I got out of the car
Stood behind it for a minute as she sat there
Watched her slide over to the driver's seat
She drove out of the parking lot without waving
Without getting out of the car
To come apologize or comfort me
I ran after her
Catching her a few car lengths away at the stop sign and
Jumped into the car
Where she had been sitting before I got out
Feeling angry and hurt I said
"So you're just going to leave like that?"
"I have to get Sarah"

Her tone was flat and resigned

I got out of the car knowing this was true
She rolled down the window and said
"I will call you"
I shrugged my shoulders and said
"I have my phone worker coming and a meeting"
She shrugged her shoulders
"Try anyway" I said and she left

Back in the office I felt like crying
Feelings of such sadness smothering me
The strong centered times just past
So blurred I did not see them

I realized I needed to run home
To get stereo speakers for our meeting
At home I wanted to collapse in bed and cry
But also did not want to

I returned to the office thirty minutes before our meeting
In time to give a new phone script to Diana
The phone worker with a creative vocabulary
And sat wondering if Ari would call

I started to hook up the speakers
So we could listen to a sales training tape
Then I discovered I had not brought the needed cables

I drove by Sarah's piano studio on my second trip home
Saw Ari's car
Saw Ari's lovely derriere as she stood beside the car
Stretching into the backseat reaching for something

I pulled half into the stall next to her
She got back into her car without looking
I walked up and saw Sally in the front seat beside Ari
With math homework spread on her lap

Turned back in disappointment and fear
That Sally would see me
Then turned around again
Adjusting to the situation and feeling silly

I said something casual
They both looked up surprised happy and smiling
Ari's smile was reserved
"How come you're here?" Sally said
"I was on my way home to get a speaker cord
   For a six o'clock meeting at work and
   I saw your car then saw your Mom's okole
   Sticking half out of the backdoor"
Sally laughed
"You're late for your meeting" Ari said
"It's okay
   Bob said he would wait for me"
"Why don't you get in"
"I don't think I want to
   I think I want to stand out here in the rain"
"It's raining?" Sally said sitting up to look
"Come in out of the rain" Ari said
"Maybe I want to stand in the rain
   Maybe I deserve to stand in the rain"
"How come?" Sally asked scrunching up her nose
"Maybe because I got angry with someone
   I deserve to stand in the rain"
"Who'd you get angry with?" Sally asked
Scooted halfway down onto the floor to look up at me
"Don't ask such personal questions" Ari told Sally
"It's okay
   She's just curious and she's my friend" I said
Sally nodded her head in full agreement
"I got angry with a friend instead of saying what I felt"

For the next ten minutes Ari and I talked in half disclosure
Twice being able to say what we meant
First when Sally was getting something to drink

Then after Sarah joined us and the girls got in the car first
And Ari walked to my car door to say goodbye

She told me she was angry at what I said
I said "Sometimes truth is hard to hear"
Still feeling contrails of anger and righteousness
She said I was being judgmental
I agreed
I told her what I had felt from her with Mamilani
She said she was just being neutral
That she had not had time to ask extra questions
She said
"You could have told me this in a kinder constructive way"
I agreed completely
Then she said
"Sorry to make you spend time with such garbage"
"Now you are sinking into self-pity"
"You're right
  It's so hard not to be reactive"
"Especially when someone you trust is unkind to you" I said
We looked into each other's eyes without speaking
Sally jumped out of their car and came over
Snuggling around her mother's waist grinning at me
We said goodbye and I left
Very late for my meeting but feeling lighter

Three hours later when I got home
My depression was back
Knowing I had blamed Ari for my feelings
I paid bills and went to bed

Unable to find the golden thread
I knew was running next to me
I lay in darkness
Wondering why I wanted to hold onto my pain
Knowing it was up to me to open to the light
So I could find the elusive golden thread
Spirit weaves through daily events

And follow it out of my darkness

SHE COMES TO YOU FOR LOVE

The next morning I gave Rich my overview of
What had happened the day before with Ari
Then read my recent dreams

In the first dream I was Ari's father
Taking her to her grandmother's who had just died
"When I recorded this in the middle of the night
I had a strong sensation I was her father in a past life"
I told Rich then went on

"In the second dream Ari and I were lovers in a foreign land
Being kept in an empty house by government troops
For our own protection during civil unrest
She went out to get some food
I followed to look after her and to see what was happening
I was about to ask her to get some food for me
When I realized she only had enough money
For food for herself"

Rich and I discussed my nurturing roll today with Ari
How it may be built on past-life experiences
"So many relationships are" Rich said then asked
"What does the second dream mean to you?"
"It tells me Ari is giving me all she can
She needs all her energy to take care of herself"
"Yes
And there's another subtle parallel you might look at
From what you have told me here and
During the course of our friendship
You were in very rough shape when you came on The Path
Right?"
"Very"

"Your freedom was greatly restricted because of the
Situation you created for yourself

"Try to look at Ari in the same light
Her restrictions from freedom are self-made
They are falling away but it takes time
Gaining spiritual freedom can happen in a moment
If we are ready
Or over lifetimes if we are not
Each of us has the right to go at our own pace
And we both know our outer circumstances follow our inner
Right?"

"Yes
That's a great comparison
I haven't looked at Ari in that light
I am still hampered physically
Living here in Hawaii I am able to appear normal
Until someone gets to know me and finds out
How easily I get chilled when it's windy and under 85
And how easily getting chilled leads to a resurgence
Of the viral symptoms I seem to carry with me
Thank you
I hope I can keep this perspective"

"You said you had three dreams
What about the third?" Rich asked

I read
"I had moved the long way from Indiana to Hawaii
Hawaii was an ever-changing party by a pool
With a lot of games
Ethel was in there
And Sharon McKinstry from a long time ago
Throwing something around in a regular way
Which then became crazy

"I heard my father had been at the pools
But he wasn't able to play
He was very much left behind when all the play started

"I heard somehow he was charged with murder and
I couldn't do anything about it
He was so far away
Way back in Indiana
He was going to be executed
But he wouldn't quite be executed
He would still be trapped in Evansville
Without his body but with a sense of hovering around
I knew I could go see him
But going back would be a horrible experience

"I woke up still asleep
Feeling anguish he was going to have this done to him
It would be all over the papers
I was so far away but would still probably read
A little blurb in the papers here
That he was put to death and
I couldn't do anything about it
I felt so bad being so far away
I couldn't do anything about it
I couldn't do anything about it"

I sat in silence feeling the dream again
Feeling grief over my father swirl around me

"This dream had a lot of impact on you" Rich said
"Yes
The murder and execution in the dream
It's so close to the way it happened
He murdered himself
On some level I know he has to pay for that karma
I know he is still stuck
He is still having his troubles"

"Yes I can feel that too
And you feel so badly about what happened to him"

The tears came from below my heart

Bursting out in deep sobs
Unable to push away grief over my father
I sat in Rich's office and cried for a long time

"You are sad you couldn't help him aren't you?"
"Yes" I whispered
"You really wanted
To take him with you on your spiritual journey"
"Yes" I almost screamed
"Feeling the pain of leaving him behind swamp me"
"And you want to do that with Ari
You want to take her with you on your spiritual path"

"Oh yes
So much"
"And you are afraid she won't be able to come
Like you father
Afraid you will have to leave her behind"

"OOOhhhh" I moaned and felt the pain wash over me
My fear of leaving her pounding inside me
When the hurt subsided I said
"It seems silly you know
I know I cannot take anyone with me
Not Dad or Ari or anyone
No one can"

"That's true
But we can each take our inner guide with us"
"Yes I forget that
I know the Mahanta is with me whenever I open to look"
"So he must be there all the time
Right?"
"I guess so
Does a tree make any sound when it falls in the forest
And no one is there to hear it?" I said and laughed
Rich laughed and I lightened though still feeling very tender

"I understand that I want to take someone special with me
Must be a deep need I haven't unraveled yet
When I feel so sad I shut off from the Mahanta
As soon as I open to him I feel better
But I am so tired of pushing the sadness away "

"Yes
You may have to feel the sadness to let it go
You can invite the Mahanta and the Light and Sound
Into your sadness
You don't have to push them away because you hurt"

"You are so right
Of course"

"Why do you think the Mahanta gave you this dream now?"

"It feels like an Alka Seltzer being dipped into water
Then removed
A little bit is released into the water
Bubbling away"

"The water image is very important for healing
Let's HU
Okay?"

Soon after beginning to sing HHHHUUUUU
My mind got stuck on Friday
Thinking about not telling Ari about my schedule
In the middle of these thoughts
Rich said gently I was on one tone and needed to relax

During the HU Rich helped me relax and open
I felt myself go deeper into contemplation
Deeper than I have in quite a while
I could feel the Light and hear a strong inner Sound
But my mind was soon going off on another tangent

We ended the HU with a soft "May The Blessings Be"

Rich told me about massaging his son's physical body
Because of adhesions his stiff little body develops
In his work on the inner with Matty he said he also
Works to massage him and limber his inner bodies
Because his son is rigid with fear from his disability

He said during our HU he had watched Spirit
Pour a beautiful lemon yellow light
Onto the joints of the inner body he sees frozen in me
How those joints are begging to limber
Though they are still stiff and creaky

I left Rich's office feeling lighter
But still with the sadness
Understanding what was happening the day before
When I became upset with Ari
How I had lost patience and perspective with her

I know it is a many year process with her
I thought how silly it felt
To be anxious over her leaving for a couple of days
When I knew she must go through
So many cycles and experiences in the years ahead

I remembered Rich's words about Ari
"She comes to you for love
  She does her contemplations for love
  She goes to the center for love
  Then she goes back to her work with her family
  To work on her karma"

KIND NECESSARY & TRUE

I went straight to work from Rich's office but
Was not effective for at least an hour
Shifting from emotional catharsis
To the mostly mental demands of our business

Late in the afternoon I ate a delayed lunch
Then went home for a quick nap
Before going back to work for the evening

My message machine played back Ari's voice telling me
She would be coming down to the shop after it closed tonight
To set up a new display for shirts
She would either call me or stop by on her way
She sounded clear

I could not call her but I did call the Malanos
To convince Mr. Malano
I needed to be there as early as possible
We had planned to go over the new contract
From the commissioner
About the time Ari was now going to stop by my apartment
The signed paperwork had to be delivered the next morning
To stop the auction
Which Mr. Malano wanted
Believing a higher bid possible

I returned to work without my nap
Left a note for Diana
So she could start her telephone work without me there
Raced through thinning rush hour to Ewa Beach
Read the contract word by word with the Malanos
Discussed the unpredictable parts of the financing
Their large negative cash flow from other income properties
Preventing best-interest rate loans
Then raced back to the office just as Diana was leaving

I flew the few blocks home
Happy to find no message on the machine
Telling me Ari was still on her way
I took a shower and was ready
To help Ari set up the new shelving

She did not come
I tried to take a nap
She still had not arrived
The dull pain I had been feeling all day
Became more pointed
I worked to stay open on the inner

I called her shop
Ari was not there but I grew confused
Finding her worker answering the phone
An hour after closing time
Finally Ari walked into my apartment

A little numb I hugged her gently
Not wanting to rush into intimacy
She was more than a little reserved
We laid down on my bed
I asked if she wanted to take off her clothes
She said "No!"
I could feel her anger and distance
She put her arms around me but her touch was hesitant
I asked what she was feeling
"Anger"
"Why are you here?"
"I don't know
   Some part of me wanted to see you"

I did not panic knowing she needed space
Needed to go through what she had to go through
I reminded myself
How judgmental I had been
How what I had said about the consciousness

She had with Robert
Was not kind
Was not necessary
I thought my words were mostly true
But probably not in the extreme way I had described it
Completely missing that point that one out of three
Does not justify the comment
Any comment
Is it kind necessary and true?
A principle of uplifting communication

She still laid against me in silence
I ask if she wanted to know what was happening with me
What was behind my upsetting words to her the day before

She talked about something else for a minute then asked
"What was behind what you said yesterday?"

I read the dream to her about my father
Described my session with Rich
Telling about feeling so much old pain from
Not being able to help my father
Feeling my deep need
For him to come with me on my spiritual path
That I wanted her to come with me too

I talked about the lesson that
No one can take anyone with them on their spiritual path
Except the Mahanta who is there anyway
I talked about struggling with this principle
While rocking with fear that I would lose her as I lost him

She talked about our differences
How she was seeing them as greater than before
She spoke in a flat tone curled into herself
She said she can just go on with her struggle by herself
I could tell she was closed off
"You're in self-destruct and flirting with self-pity"

I said trying to jolt her awake
"No I am not"
I mentioned her mood again a little later with tact
She did not deny as strongly

Her low self-image flared
She talked about not wanting to hold me back
Not wanting to inflict
The garbage of their consciousness on me

I told her
"I know the principle of listening to a good friend
  Who is having trouble in a relationship
  Who wants to confide those troubles

"It's great to listen
  But if I say the same negative things
  About the friend's spouse or significant other
  My friend will get very angry with me and
  Defend the relationship he criticized a moment ago

"I know I violated that principle with you
  If I had put it into different words
  The things you have told me
  About your relationship with Robert
  I think they would be worse than what I said yesterday

"That does not change the principle I ignored
  It doesn't excuse me
  And there might be some truth in what I said"

"You could have been nice about what you said"
She dug her elbow into my ribs

"Yes I sure could have and
  I'm sure there are lots of things that go on
  In your relationship with Robert which are uplifting
  Which are full of love

It is not the darkness that I painted it to be yesterday
When I was hurting and unable to say to you
'I feel so lost
I feel so hopeless'"

She warmed up
I warmed up
Our hearts met
We made love warmly and very closely

I felt the budding of independence
Perhaps only momentary

I shared with Ari I had told Rich about her two dreams
In which I was dead
"He shares the point of view
That you know best what your dreams mean
He said usually with his patients who are working to unfold
Death in the dream state means a change in consciousness
He thought it could mean
The consciousness she has had with me is changing
Which is needed for the relationship to mature"

We went to her shop very late
Laughing and joking as we rearranged the shirts
She dropped me home but did not want to leave
I kissed her good night for the fortieth time
After I got out of the car
She told me playfully to not look at another woman
That I was hers

I canceled my comeback that she needed to be fully mine
Before she could ask that of me
Because I did not want to feel her drawn back into her realty
Taking back what she had said

She must have heard my thoughts
She told me as I leaned in through the car door window

How Robert had hugged her recently
When neither of them were being sexual
Warmly hugged her like he used to
And almost said something to her
She had asked him what he was about to say
Then quoted him
"I was going to say I wish you were all mine
  But I know you are not and I did not want to hurt you"
"What did you feel when he said that?"
"I wished I could be all his
  But I am not"
"It must tear at you sometimes
  Having two men who both want you all to themselves
  Feeling you would like to grant both our wishes"

I watched her drive away in the night
Disappearing down the wet street

LOVE AND TRUST AND LOSS

"When I am angry with you
You are hurt because I am not showing you love
You feel junk inside because
I am showing you anger instead of love

"Do you think I love you any less when I am angry with you?

"Well I don't love you any less
But you don't know it
Because I am not showing you I love you
When you are at home doing whatever and
Thinking about me and missing me and
Feeling a lot of love for me
Do you think I know it?
Do you think I feel it?

"The great love on the inner between us
You spoke about Friday is there
We also have a love on the outer
We have senses which operate only on the outer
If this were not true
The physical world would not be anything like it is
And you would not need to be with your family
You could just love them on the inner

"I know you think that is different
That's why I talking about this right now
You love me in part because I show you love
I take the risks to make myself vulnerable
I go outside myself to go to you
Protected only by the trust that you love me
And the willingness to feel exposed and
To deal the best I can with whatever you give back to me

"Sometimes you give silence back to me

"I see our relationship difficulties arising
From two basic realities
Yours is that you love me and you love Robert and
You want to be with us both
And you have a hard time handling your feelings
Which come up around this
Mine is that I love you and I want to be with you
And I have a hard time handling my feelings
Which come up around this

"I see several similarities and one basic difference
In our difficulties
The similarities are we both have chosen it
We both have difficulty handling our feelings and
We both want something we are not getting

"The basic differences
Is that you want to be with both Robert and me
I want to be with only you
I do not have a wife and family I also want to be with
Who I am with when I am not with you

"If I did I would go out of my way
To make you feel loved continually
By showing it in numerous big and little ways

"If I just stayed with my feelings
Of intense love and longing for you and
Saw you whenever I could
I would know
No matter how loving I was to you
When I was able to see you
You would not feel loved much of the rest of the time
Because of your pain that I was with someone else and
Because I was not showing you love at those times

"This is the heart of many of my upsets with you
The ways I have suggested you might show me love

You either agree with and rarely do
Or you tell me you don't see why they would be necessary
As you did Friday night

"You have said
'Saying I love you and miss you
The first thing on the phone is just not me'
Of course it is not you
If it were you
You would be doing it already
Anything we learn to do is not us before we learn it
You have such great love and trust for me
You don't think it's necessary
To say I love you when first on the phone but
You almost always say it near the end of the conversation
You almost always say it when we are together
Though usually not when we first meet

"Do you remember what you asked me last week about Robert?
You asked me
'Could a man have so much love and not show it?'
You did not know if he loved you
Or how much he loved you because he did not show it
You are no better than Robert
I am no better than Robert
Robert is no better than anybody else
But you are drawn to me to experience some things
You have not experienced with Robert

"This principle will make your marriage better
If you will only learn it and apply it
Remember what every psychic told you years ago?
'You will have two men in your life
The second will make your marriage stronger'

"The principle in the physical world is
Love is communicated by showing
Showing love is what makes people feel loved

Saying what you feel is the next best way to show love
Both are necessary to communicate love fully

"Feeling love makes the person loving feel good
It can be felt by the person being loved
But not nearly as much
As the love communicated by loving actions
Not nearly as much as spoken words of tenderness

"You show love to your girls all the time
In the way you care for them
Do you think they would feel as loved by you
If you did not help them get ready
For whatever they have to face in their young lives?
If you never fixed them breakfast
Do you think they would feel as loved by you?

"When you are in my arms
You are showing me your love for me
But that is not enough by itself for me
Because you are so often not in my arms

"Would you know I loved you if every time you came over
I said 'Hi' then kept writing
Only stopping to get a glass of water and
Give you a quick hug after an hour
Then merely saying good-bye when you left?
You might handle it for a while
But soon you would tire of it
You would tire of my ignoring you
Because I was not giving you enough love to keep you going
I was not showing you love by spending time with you

"Simply being in my arms a few hours a week and
Feeling your love for me when you are not with me
Is not enough to make me always feel you love me
Because I have an aching child who needs reassurance
Which is my job

And because you want to keep your marriage alive
And be lovers with me at the same time
Which is your responsibility

"The way I shower you with the little actions of love
An outsider might think I was the one
Who wanted to have my wife and you too

"I do this because it is something I have learned
I think it is one of the big reasons
You love me like you do
So when you tell me as you did Friday night on the phone
That you don't feel it is necessary to take the first step
To open a conversation by saying I love you and I miss you
To offer me reassurance when you are not around
Because of the deep trust we have and because it is not you
I say you feel the deep trust because
I am always available to you
Always loving if I am not upset because you are not around
You are rarely available to me when I want you
Every time I see you
I hold my breath wondering if this will be the time
You tell me Robert has raised a new kind of ruckus and
You can't see for awhile
Or forever

"I don't feel like you acknowledge by your actions
This basic difference in our experience
I feel really hurt when you say to me in action or words
You don't think it is necessary
To do the little things I have asked you to do
Or to find other ways to tell me you still love me
To help me through my hurt and pain
Over you being with your husband"

This is what I wanted to say to Ari
Wanted to say so badly I wrote it first and took it with me
To meet her before Sunday Service

Determined not to get angry with her
But she would not read my words
She was upset because I had acted upset the night before
When she would not come upstairs
For thirty seconds
To get a print-out of sample typefaces for signs for her shop
Leaving Sarah asleep in the car with the new baby-sitter
Who was almost asleep
Giving us the chance to hug as lovers
For the first time in four days
Something she had suggested and we had done
During the early summer in a similar circumstance

She was not open to my attempt to say what I had written
I pressed my point sinking low feeling her resistance
Feeling so drained from my week of inner and outer challenges
Which I had alluded to
But not yet been able to share with her
As I kept pressing her to learn this awareness
To accept my view or propose her own solution
She became angry saying
She could not handle the ups and downs anymore
We slowly escalated
Me pressing intently without becoming angry
She resisting becoming very angry

I tried to tell her I needed her help
I tried to ask her to help me

She would not accept she wanted to be with both Robert and me
Unable to see the difference between
Her feelings and her actions

She would not agree that love needs
To be spoken and shown in actions
Not just felt

She was squirming in her seat so hard

I knew she would have gotten out if we were in my car
"Do you want me to leave" I said
"Yes" she spat out

So l got out and left
I was not angry
I had to let her go
I could not run after her to apologize
I was in my crisis of loss and
I needed the acknowledgment from her
She could help if she choose to

I drove home with only small tugs to run away
Drove home in tears splattering like projectile vomit
Feeling my world was collapsing
Knowing I would stay with my feelings no matter what came
Not knowing what would come

At home I fell onto my bed and cried
I got up to take out my contact lenses
Turned on my computer instead and began writing
Wondering how many days it would be before she called
Wondering how I would be able to manage work the next day
Wondering how I could live without her
Knowing I would have to
If she chose to block learning
Chose not to counter with
"I cannot do what you ask but I can try to do this"

Hunger for learning is the foundation of any relationship for me

Tears continued to erupt but I wrote
A beautiful Sunday morning outside
Light pouring into my white apartment
Competing with my grief

Then she was there
Standing in the doorway to my study

Looking Sunday fresh carrying a bouquet of sadness
I looked into her eyes
As she walked to me saying
"I don't want to be without you"
"I don't either" I said and my heart exploded
Grief and pain already rumbling from my work with Rich
Rolled over her and over me
As she held me while I sat in my writing chair

I cried like I cried laying on the floor in the funeral home
After everyone had left
Leaving me alone with my father's body
Lying in his casket with his death mask of pain
An arm's length away from me

I cried and cried in Ari's arms
Saying through gasps at one point
"I
   Hurt
   So
   Much"

Later I got out "I just want a little help"
Then "No one ever helps me"
To which I added
"I know that is not true
   But it seems that way"
When my tears dried
She said she had wanted to run away from everything
She told me she was sorry she had been so silly
To not see what was happening with me
To not ask me what had happened this week
She said she had read what I wrote
"I really do want to learn"
"I know you do" I said stroking her hair

We held each other as closely as we possibly could
In our impossibly awkward position of

Me sitting and her half kneeling to put herself at my level

"What did happen this week?" she asked

I took a deep breath and said
"Wednesday afternoon after our late night together Tuesday
 I came home for a nap and just as I closed my eyes
 Laureen called
 She was going through a crisis
 I was able to help her
 But unable to get any rest
 Before going back to work for the evening

"The next morning at 5:00 my sister Jan called
 Very upset over Mother
 I was able to help her
 To get out of the way and let Spirit help her
 Sharing with her what Rich and I have been working on
 With my Mother stuff
 But I did not get back to sleep

"Later that morning I again took the question of
 Remaining Local Director into contemplation
 And was so clearly shown I need to
 'clean out my outer commitments at the Center'
 So I did"

"When did you resign?"

"Thursday morning
 I felt such a loss
 When you serve Spirit in a role like that
 There is an extra boost coming though
 I felt it two years ago when I took the job
 It's okay
 I am more connected on the inner now
 But I will have to make more of the connection myself

"Some of my experiences over the past three or four years
Have piled up
And with what Laureen went through
I have lost my trust in the local Path leadership
The feeling of loss has been tremendous this week
I know that at some point
I must be willing to give up everything
To fully surrender all my attachments and
Completely let Spirit decide
What I do and do not have in my life

"And today I thought you were gone"

I sobbed on Ari's shoulder
When I stopped she asked me
"What happen to Laureen"

"I am not supposed to tell anyone
She told me in confidence" I said
Knowing I would tell her
Knowing I had to share what I was going through with her
"You can tell me" Ari said softly

"Please understand that The Path is an outer organization
Its main value is as a doorway to the inner
One of the doorways
People make up the organization
People with unescapable human consciousnesses
No matter how unfolded they are
Being on the physical means
Dealing with the positive and negative for all of us
Within ourselves and all-around"

"Yes I know"

"As within any organization
Some people make good decisions
Some do not

Some make both kinds
Ethyl has told Laureen
She cannot do Sunday Services anymore
Has told her she is out of touch with The Path

"I have gotten to know Laureen quite well
She is often opinionated
She is swept around by deep feelings
She does not always handle
But I have never experienced
One moment of deception with her
She is who she is and
She is ferociously dedicated to Spirit
No one I know asks for guidance more than she
Nor is as willing to follow what she hears on the inner"

"She is a long way from perfect
But I find her heart true
I cannot say the same thing for Ethyl
More and more I see the darkness around her
And I am no longer able to brush off
The way she has treated me at times
Some of which I have told you"

"Yes I remember"

"So I have lost the feeling of family
I have cherished at the Center
I can no longer talk freely with Sandy and Colleen
For they are a direct pipeline to Ethyl
They are wonderful hearts
But they are too open with Ethyl about what I say

"Please do not let my experience
Color your view of the Center or of Ethyl
The higher we each go on The Path
The more light and love we find
And the more darkness we become aware of

It is just a part of being on the physical

"Knowing about too much darkness
Before opening enough to light and sound
Can set someone back
Please look at this as my experience
Please look at what has happened between Laureen and Ethyl
As happening between them
Laureen knows she has had a role in causing this
There was a time when Ethyl reached out to her and
Laureen rebuffed her
Since then Laureen has been rebuffed by Ethyl
When she has reached out

"Ethyl does a lot of good
She spreads a lot of Spirit around
She also has her dark side as we each do
Please please keep this in mind"

We spent the rest of our time together locked in passion
On my unmade bed
Bathed in sunshine and white light
Before having a quick late lunch of Thai food and
Lingering over our good-bye kisses
So much love flowing between us
Each of us renewed for a while longer
To handle the pain we feel when apart

Then she said "I need to go home"

I WOULD NOT MIND

As Ari left Sunday
The desperation felt completely gone
She said she had felt my pain when we were making love
And it was still there with her
Though lessened

I stood in the elevator with her
To go the one-story down to the parking lot
Getting a final hug she cannot give me if we go down the stairs
Then watched her drive off

I struggled to balance myself
Reeling from the casual comment she had to get home
To do some work before going out to dinner that night
Jealousy raging through me
My scorn of her social outing
Narrowing to a sniper's red dot

I took a breath then thought to myself
"Zak if you were happy with your life
 With being by yourself
 With your work and writing and inner work
 Would you mind what Ari did when she was not with you"
I answered myself in a heartbeat
"No
 I would not mind"
With that awareness I dropped my jealousy
And spent the rest of the afternoon and evening
Doing laundry
Writing
Reading Michener's *The Novel*
Then a book on revising fiction
Listening to a tape of HU songs
Recorded at several major Seminars

That evening after Ari left

Sitting at the computer
I reread the letter I had written to Sri Thomas
Telling him why I had resigned as local director
Also telling him I was troubled with some energy
I felt in the local community
Described some of the things I had experienced with Ethyl

I printed out the letter
Set it on my desk and
Began working on other writing
I felt a dark presence in the kitchen and became hyper-aware
The presence felt like Ethyl
The target of the energy was the letter
I got up and locked the door
And felt better

And went to bed clear and open
After doing a spiritual exercise before sliding under the covers
Laying in the pool of spiritual energy
Not resenting being kept awake

Remembering Rich's words about the parallel
Between Ari going back to her family to do her work
Unable to yet be free of her karma
Just like I was unable to be free
Of my body's self-created restrictions
When I first found The Path

The next morning
I was writing again
The letter sitting still sitting on my desk
I felt Ethyl's partner's presence
And dark energy directed toward the letter
I had no issues with Allen
But writing my experiences was important
I made a copy of my back-up disks and
Put them out to take to work
Once I put the letter to Sri Thomas

In an addressed envelope with a stamp
Then set it out to mail
The energy cleared

WITH RICH BUSH CLINTON AND PEROT

I spent the first half an hour recapping my current events
Rich felt there was a lot of movement in my awareness
In the elevator aware my uncomfortableness with Ari's social involvement
Was because I was not comfortable being alone
Being without
Being with myself
We talked about the two psychic attacks
I described the two events
I wondered if they were paranoia
He said "No go with your inner" forget your mind

I went over my dreams

We did a HU
Rich began speaking gently
"I can see what you mean
   There is dark psychic stuff around you
   You have surrounded yourself
   With white light protecting yourself"

He reminded me I was holding
Controlling the pain in my gut
He said
"As you are able to let go of the control
   You will be able to let Spirit and the Mahanta in to heal

After we came out he talked about how he saw
The white light and the dark psychic force around me
How it came as a huge dark wave and
Rose up over me
In his mind he had yelled
"Oh No not to Zak"
But he calmed his thoughts and watched as the dark wave
Sliced through the light
Sliced me in half

Then he saw the white light of Spirit
Come into and mix with the black and become grey
"The psychic energy that is being directed
Toward you is serving Spirit too
No matter what the intentions of those sending it
It is helping break up your inner blocks
When you try to control and hold onto your fear
You are like the boy putting his fingers into the dike
Spirit wants you to learn to swim in the sea
No matter what comes
To swim with Spirit and the Mahanta
With the attitude of
Whatever comes to me will wash away and
I will be better for it"

We talked about spiritual leadership
I said could feel myself entering a period of
Intense inner work
Of putting my leadership role in the outer on hold
But what I was doing was part of my growing

Rich agreed and said
"There is a great need for spiritual leadership
On the inner as well
The inner worlds are outer worlds too
Just different outer worlds"

After our session
I asked Rich what he did with his notes
He said he used them to
Help him remember key points and
Sometimes he doodled
He did not review them unless medication was involved
He said he had the kind of mind that remembered people's
Dreams and their experiences very well
But he had a hard time with details
I said you must have had a hard time with medical school
He said

"No
  My ex-wife used to kid me that I did not study
  Only slept on my books"
He said he could not learn by rote
He learned on the inner
He was aware of reviewing the material in his dreams
He had trouble during the first two years working in hospitals
Because he is so sensitive
Being around people who hurt so much and
Had so much illness was difficult for him to block out

I asked him if I had drained him
When we talked about mortgages last week
He said
"No
  Those were details which are a part of life
  I am drained by people who go off on mental tangents
  Explaining mental theories
  That aren't relevant to life today
   as they or I experience it"

We talked about politics
How he had enjoyed watching Perot
"Better for me than Saturday Night Live" he said
I shared with him that Laureen
Had been watching one of the debates and
Had gone to inner to see what she could learn

She learned Bush was asleep
Clinton had his heart open and
Perot did not have his heart open
Even though he was saying the right words
I said what a wonderful way to look at the political process

He agreed and said it is time to move on from the Bush world
He said Clinton is the one
Who has the energy ideas and an open heart
Rich said he has really enjoyed watching Perot

Shake up the process
By bringing economic realities into the picture

ANOTHER SAD SUNDAY

Running myself into the ground
First too worn out to work well
Then a bug emptied my energy
More pushing
My energy on staccato
Too worn out to write
Then to think
Disappointment Saturday night upset me
Upset Ari
I soothed her for hours
She left okay
Woke up the next morning down
After worship service
She could not handle my pain and fears
We fought
She got angry saying I give her suggestions all the time
But I reject hers
Tell her she does not understand
I told her that day when she had delivered her suggestion
On the point of anger
It hurt
She denied doing so
Said again I don't listen to her
That I want her to talk more
But when she does
I tell her to shut up by not listening
I said I had not heard about this before
She said I do it all the time
I felt she was hurt and was
Throwing anything she could at me
Like I do to her sometimes
Often

We parted on an unhappy note
I sat with my pain all afternoon
Finally becoming angry at her

She came by an hour later
I told her she asks me
To put up with her difficult situation all the time but
When my situation gets difficult she folds her tent
She said she was apprehensive to see me lately
Never knowing how I would be

On and on
She was ready to end our relationship
She did not respond to my tears or hugs
She told me how hard she works to see me
How her work is never done right these days
I said how no one could do all the work she is trying to do
She said Sally went to school a few days ago
Unprepared for a test that day
Because Ari had not been there to help her the night before
Sally's class is getting into fractions earlier than other classes and
She needed Ari's help
Ari said it broke her heart
To see her little girl go off to school unprepared for the test

That got through to me
I held her
Brushed her head
Agreed with her how she must feel frustrated and hurt
She broke down

An hour later she left with her cheeks dried
Her eyes hollow
The traces of a smile on her lips
We had agreed not to end our relationship that night
I told her I would be more understanding
I would handle my pain better

She showed up again at ten o'clock in the evening
On her way to do some late work in her store
She said she could stay for twenty minutes

More than two hours later she left
Having said at one point
Wrapped in my arms
Her clothes spread neatly on the carpet beside my futon
"It feels like after a storm
   Calm but not quite back together again"

As I watched her drive away
I could only think “Where do we go from here?”
And wonder if she was thinking the same

EXTRAMARITAL THERAPY

The storm passed
Another threatening on the horizon
I called Rich and asked him
About Ari joining us for a session
"Usually I see both people separately
  Then together, then alternating
   As we all decide
   Your situation is so intense
   I would leave it up to Ari
   If she wants to come
   Then yes I would see you both"

Ari said yes surprising me

In the middle of November
Mid-morning
On Friday the thirteenth
We joked about avoiding black cats
As we drove to Rich's Office
After Ari picked me up

I was determined not to talk too much
Ari was nervous about opening up
I thought I would get some things validate
About her opening up

She was wonderfully poised
Posing her questions clearly
I was vulnerable and hurting

One of her questions
"When a hurt is taken inside what is the difference between
   Digesting it
   Letting it go
   And stuffing it?"

I worked to be neutral
Wanting to give her space to talk
Rich helped a lot

"Quite a difference in terms of impact
   Digesting takes a strong base to sit with discomfort
   Letting a hurt go can come next
   If it no longer serves a purpose in a person's life
   Those who bury their hurts deep inside
   Usually are giving too much of themselves to others
   Shortchanging their own nourishment"

Rich stopped for a moment to look at his notes
I looked at Ari
She was watching Rich, who then spoke again
"Someone who stuffs their hurts
   Will reach a point where they need to let it go
   Some explode
   It's a process though
   Exploding will create a backlash
   Finding constructive ways to vent our hurts
   Is the one key to our personal growth
   The less someone leans on another person
   When venting
   The deeper the healing
   And the stronger they become as a person

"I see people drawn together sharing joy
   Then they get down to the unfinished sides of themselves
   Sharing their rougher edges
   Sharing their pain
   Often without embracing their personal responsibility
   Losing the upward momentum in the relationship
   Created by sharing joy and love
   Some people try to turn their relationship
   Into a therapeutic relationship
   I have yet to see one work
   Instead they go downhill"

Rich's words hit home for me
Highlighting a part of my history

I found myself feeling hopeless
Staring in the eye of what I thought was my last out
Of my last at-bat

Wanting validation that expressing feeling is important
Wanting support in creating an environment with Ari
Where she would share more feelings and more pain
So I could share my pain

Sharing feelings is really important
Learning not to expect caretaking
Not to look for the other person to fix it or make it better
This is what Spirit is for
This is what I am for…for myself

Rich's words of truly embracing responsibility
For my own feelings
Echoed through me

Rich used the analogy of our relationship being a child
We have created
Who grows and is nurtured
Depending on the kind of food we feed it
When together or a part
Feeding the child pain will stunt it
Feeding it the wonder and adventure of our love
Will help the child grow

"Taking care of each of ourselves" Rich said
"Is the foundation of all our relationships
  Love means giving freedom"

I heard all this
Agreed

And felt lost
Because I did not know how to do it

Hurting so much in our relationship with Ari
Confusing my old hurts and new hurts
Staring at the prospect of not seeing her
Far more hurtful than anything I could experience with her

She talked about her fears
About getting more involved with me
About her struggle to reconcile her love for me with
What has been unthinkable
Her unquestioned desire to keep her family together
Providing a broken home for her kids is just not an option

So we left
I think she had a lot of clarity and I had a lot of pain
I saw I could not get away with it anymore
I had been manipulating her in subtle ways
Trying to have her get in my pain with me
I felt shitty seeing what game I was playing

I went to Rich's thinking about validation
I did not get invalidated
But I got a light shown in the direction
I had been avoiding
I see a need step then avoid it

I thought about how I lean on the Mahanta
When I can clear my focus
Which works for a while
Then I shift to Ari
Looking for her to take care of me
As I slide off my discipline of surrendering to the Mahanta

Walking out of the building with Ari
My pager went off as we passed a payphone
It was Laureen checking on me

After I had seen her the previous day
When I was feeling so much pain
I returned her call and briefly summed up what
I had learned in the session with Rich
And for her to say
How taking care of each of ourselves takes discipline
Takes constant effort to do the things which helps us grow and
To choose not to do the things which pull us down
As often as we can

Her words were just what I needed at that moment
Reminding me I had slipped into a place of
Wanting what I wanted
Instead of working to grow and be a better vehicle for Spirit

The rest of the afternoon I spent with Ari
She felt a little distant to me and more with herself
I did not pull at her
Saying to myself
"I can do this
  I really want to do this
  I really want to take care of myself
  It's hard
  But that's okay
  I take care of my feelings
  The Mahanta is always there if I need help"
It worked for a while

Rich had said each time
I find someone
Some activity
Something outside myself
To produce a new feeling
To take away the pain
Covering over what I am feeling in the moment
Rich said every time I do this
I pour syrup on my anthill
My feelings get stuck in the sticky sweet diversions and

I am not able to unfold spiritually
Until I work free of the syrup

THANKSGIVING

On the phone two days later
Ari invited me to come to their home
For Thanksgiving dinner
Her tone was muted dread
Neither of us fully open and loving
The obvious land mines of my joining them for a holiday meal
Eager for our footfalls
And resulting explosions

I resisted
She resisted too saying it was Robert's idea
I freaked silently
Then pried myself open to the inner
Seeing that if Robert could invite me
Into his home with grace
I could at least go with grace and
Maybe even share some love

The meal turned out to be a defused
Few hours of dulled near fun
Ari's and my dampened passions
Less threatening to Robert and the girls
Than times past full of Ari's and my electricity

SODA

Feeling the undercurrents of fear running softly
I waited in the car
Tired but happy
Very little viral feeling remained from what was now
A full month of the flu
The second in three months

I waited for Ari and the girls coming to Sunday Service
Relaxing with my seat tilted back
Lost in thought last anchored
By the colors of the gas station across the street
A loud bang and yell jerked me around to see
Sally grinning at me through the window
Ari and Sarah and the girl's cousin April laughed and waved
A few parking stalls away

I jumped out of the car and hugged Sal
Swinging her around
Teasing her for ambushing me
My lingering anxiety over seeing Ari
As friends not lovers washed away by love

The Service went smoothly for me
No emotional landmines
During the discussion about Detachment
Then it was over and we were on our way to lunch
I discouraging any expectation of seeing Ari as I wanted
Another Bali trip just two days away
Ari and I alone for eleven days
Flying from Paradise with complication
To Paradise without

The three girls wanted pizza
I did not but kept quiet
On the way to the restaurant at the mall
Sarah told me she knew what I could get her for Christmas

I teased her saying
"I am getting you something for Christmas?"
I asked the other girls what I should get Sarah
Planning to ask everyone for input about everyone else
Sally said
“A Ken doll in a shiny tux”
And stuck out her tongue at her sister
April was quiet
Ari said “I think she has enough already”
Sarah said she wanted a little motorized car or diamonds and
Did not want to play this game
She wanted to talk about what she wanted
Ari and I joked about naked greed

We entered Kahala Mall through the entrance by the theaters
I mentioned "Home Alone 2" to Ari as we walked in
Knowing the kids wanted to go
From driving by another theater the night before
The same three girls screaming to see it playing there
As we took me home after the second annual
Dance in the Light and Sound held in Kapiolani Park

Ari said
"No
   The lines will be long
   Let's see what's here"

She and Sarah wanted to see "Last of the Mohicans"
Which started in forty minutes at 12:30
Sally and April wanted to see "Aladdin"
Unsure I wanted to sit through any movie
I said nothing

Ari said to the girls
"Put it to a vote"
Aladdin won
Sarah pouted
Ari said

"It does not start until 1:30
   I told Daddy we would be home by 2:00"
"We can walk home" April said
I jumped off my seat of ambivalence
If the kids stayed to see "Aladdin" by themselves
Ari could take me home
We could have a few minutes or more alone

"Aladdin" seemed to be gaining momentum
A more leisurely lunch was discussed
Ari seemed to be struggling
"I would like to see
Last of the Mohicans
   Want do you want to do?" she said to me

I looked at her in disbelief
She was sabotaging a chance to be alone
On a day when neither of us expected it
In disgust I said
"I really don't want to see it
   Any way two weeks ago you said
   It was too violent for the kids
   When we could have gone"
"I've softened on it since then"
My two-year-old saw only
She was putting a movie ahead of us being together
I closed off my heart

I did not get angry
I just withdrew and watched the scene unfold
Sarah clung to her pouting
We left the theater area
To find the restaurant the girls had chosen
Ari holding Sarah to her side talking to her
I walked slowly still feeling weak
Watching the four of them form an arms-together line
Pulling away from me with every step

Conflicting unpleasant feelings surged
I dodged
Wanting just to leave
To run away
I did not and the restaurant had a waiting line

Sarah did not cheer up
Ari announced that there would be no movie
Sally and April took it well
I took it well
Except I was already disgusted with Ari's earlier choice

We drove to another pizza restaurant
The car silent
So different from the play and joy earlier
Ari felt closed and angry
I felt closed and disgusted

At the restaurant Ari stayed with Sarah in the car
Sally and April and I went inside to get a table
Then Sally went back outside
Sensing the distress between her mother and sister
"It's hard to be happy all the time isn't it?" I said
April agreed and we talked about what kind of pizza to get
I wondered if I should eat any with my health still fragile

Ten minutes later Sarah Sally and Ari came in
Ari looked a little softer
The girls had red eyes
I squeezed both their hands

As we were ordering Ari vetoed the girls having sodas
Saying in a harsh way
There was no nutritional value in soft drinks
I thought she was being ludicrous
Objecting to sodas in a pizza place
The debate raged on with the waitress standing patiently
Finally Ari asked me what I thought

I said with a small explosion of air
"I think you are being absurd
  Talking about nutrition
  When you are getting ready to feed them this stuff
  Let the kids have the sodas"
The girls cheered
The sodas were ordered and the waitress retreated
Ari said
"I think it is a sin
  The way people who don't have much money
  Buy soft drinks by the caseload
  I don't think people on food stamps
  Should be allowed to buy sodas"

If I had been in better shape
If I had kept the Sunday Service discussion about Detachment
With me for even an hour
I would have seen Ari's distress and cajoled her out of it

If

"What else are you going to restrict?" I asked
"Just what is bad for them"
"Who is going to decide that?
  How are you going to feel when someone tells you
  What you can or cannot buy?"
"We take care of ourselves
  I think everybody should take care of themselves"
"That's easy for you to say"

Our discussion fizzled out soon
I was glad she was two seats away
After I was silent for several minutes Ari said
"Did my opinions depress you?"
"Strong opinions usually do" I answered
" Are you okay Zak?" the girls ask one at a time
"I'm fine"

A little later Ari mentioned she had too many masters
"Who's are your masters?" Sally asked
Ari hesitated then in a causal named her family members
Then said "And Zak"
I said
"I decline being anyone's master
  I can see your frustration
  You should be you own master
  Period"
"Easy for you to say" she said

On the way back to my car
I asked Ari to let me know when she felt like smiling
She grinned but with little joy

We parted in a drizzling rain
Having survived a miserable lunch with greed and attachment

1992 YEAR OF THE PASSPORT

Is my year of traveling over?
Has my time with Ari come to an end?
She says she can no longer handle my feelings
Too much of what I feel washes over her
Too much of the pain
She has yet to object to too much love

I know I am a more feeling person than she is today
I think she is a more feeling person than two years ago
She might disagree

This morning she is lying in bed with her eyes shut
Listening to a tape on her headphones
In a lot of pain because I express too much feeling
Sometimes clearly sometimes not

We are in Bali again
Our third trip this year
She has bought even more
Than our September trip here and to Bangkok

Two days and a night remain here
Then twelve hours of travel wrapped around
Another 12 hours in Guam
Then we will be home
Back to Honolulu
Ari back to her family
Seeing me occasionally
I will return to work and life alone again
Seeing her occasionally

I hope we will still see each other
Right now she is not willing or able
To handle my feelings
She says she feels caught between two strong men
Who are so set in their ways she has trouble breathing

Not an easy position for her or anyone

I am trying hard to step away from my feelings
Without stuffing them somewhere to ferment
I am not doing well enough to please Ari

We still love each other
I have yet to trust her love
Every time she goes home to Robert
Goes home trying to be as close as she can to him
I freak a little
She does not see most of my reacting
If she did we probably would not have come this far
Knowing my time with her hangs by the thread of
Robert's wish for Ari to be happy
Makes small things harder to handle

If he said to her tomorrow
"Choose him or me"
She would choose him
She would not be happy and he knows this
But she would choose her family

I am willing to live and love under these conditions
But I don't always do so gracefully

So what now?
More pain
Maybe more joy
More lessons
More time alone
The Mahanta always available
Comfort only an open heart away

Am I to live hurting so?
Is this the end of such beautiful time with Ari?

We almost made up twice since last night
If I turn to her now will she open her heart?
Will I?

FOOD FIGHT

Last night we talked about how our simple dinner in Kuta
Was so expensive for many working people in Bali
Our driver Erawan makes enough money each month
To eat like we were eating only a few evenings a month
And do nothing else

I said
"In Honolulu this would be equivalent
  To a visiting mortgage client
  Spending $500 for every dinner
  I don't know where to spend $500 for dinner
  Do you?"

The last two sentences were my first imprudence

"That's not too hard to do
  Dinner upstairs at the Halekulani
  Runs that much easily with drinks "

"Without drinks?"
"Maybe $140
  That's my favorite restaurant"

I have a button around spending large sums of money on food
Hearing others say they enjoy it makes me angry
Hearing Ari say it was her favorite restaurant
Felt intolerable at the moment
I made my second mistake by saying
"If we ever get together full time that could be an issue"
"Don't worry I won't take you"
"Who will you take
  Your next boyfriend?
  And don't expect to use my money"

She was charitable
She made it clear she would pay her own way

And she was kind enough to
Not review my ability to earn an income

We remained stuck in attack-and-parry
She told me I was being judgmental
I was
I told her she is spoiled
I still think so

We forgot about loving our differences
I reacted and she reacted to my reaction
She is doing this more and more
Having a harder time handling my emotional ups and downs
Just when I think I am doing better
Not great but better

This morning she accused me of loving my feelings
Of loving my pain
She's right
The intensity of hurting can be seductive
I have grown more aware of my pattern in the past few years
I love to feel

I love freedom more
Feeling in itself is a trap
I trap myself often
I asked her for special consideration
Because of the extreme challenge of her situation

She would not give me what I asked for
I don't know if she should or not
We both are beyond our comfort zones
Far beyond
The limits of our relationship maybe be near
I hope not

SAFE HARBOR

Back home again
Bali fading
We parted as tolerant lovers
Who struggled to love
Our physical attraction
Buffeted by high waves and
And even stronger emotional winds
Our hearts retreating
Desperate for safe harbor

WITH RICH

I had been back ten days when I saw Rich again
Slogging through a deadened recounting
Of recent events

"Let's HU" Rich finally said "See if it helps you open"

I felt myself melting under the uplifting energy of
HHHHUUUUUing
So much fell away
Icebergs of frozen feelings
Standing naked in a harsh winter's sun

"You can come in out of the cold if you wish" Rich said
"Just ask the Mahanta"

So I did
The winter sun became warm
I found myself
Sitting on a bench next to Zand
In a meadow of wildflowers
Zand looked at me and said without speaking
"Look to love first and only
   To love is to give
   And to receive
   But never to take
   When our pain is so near the surface
   It is ready to leave
   The choice is ours
   A choice we may not realize we can make
   Until we surrender to the Mahanta"

Then I was back with Rich
Looking across his small office
Into his eyes of amazing depth and sparkle
As though Zand was there inside him

I left soon after that
Having crossed a long bridge over a narrow ravine

BRUSHED LIPS

Ari stopped by the next evening
Without making plans to do so
I knew she would come
Just as I knew we both were moving on

I heard her at the door and
Hugged her warmly as she stepped into the kitchen
After a moment she pulled back gently
And said
"I have found my peace
   About what comes next and
   I hope tonight I can help you find yours"

I could see her decision in her eyes
"I am at peace" I said
"Found yesterday on the inner
   With Zand in Rich's office"

"I saw Zand too" she said
   "On the inner
   While singing HU before bed
   I must care for my family
   And myself
   With all the love I can free up
   Within myself"

We looked at each other
Lips a few inches apart but not touching
My young man standing patiently nearby
Not yelling or crying or demanding anything
I waited for Ari to say more
Finally she did
"I can't see you anymore as a lover
   Not sure I can see you at all
   Until I adjust to this
   It breaks my heart

But I literally have no choice
This is my decision
Robert and the girls
Have nothing to do with this"
She paused
"Well they have everything to do with this
But no demands have been put on me"

I hugged her again
Feeling her tenderness
Feeling my boy beginning to shake inside

We parted just a bit
Our lips almost touching
Looking into each other's eyes
"I am okay Beauty
More than okay
We both need to do this
To take our next steps
I love you forever"

Tears in our eyes she brushed my lips
Then turned and walked out of my apartment
I did not follow her to watch her drive away

About the Author

BC embraces life's adventures by focusing more on what he is doing than what he has. Relying on spiritual awareness, often called intuition, helps him to see the hidden lessons behind everyday encounters. Learning (still!) that ignoring this inner guidance often makes the road rougher to travel, he accepts opportunities to unfold however they come.

When asked about his writing, he explains, *"Forty years ago, I found I had little to write about. Ten years later, I began to develop my writer's voice."* Today BC lives in Honolulu with his lovely wife Sweetie, delving into his personal experiences and imagination through his writing.

www.ingramcontent.com/pod-product-compliance
Lightning Source LLC
LaVergne TN
LVHW091043080826
845145LV00002B/610

* 9 7 8 1 7 3 6 2 8 8 4 5 0 *